THE UNITED STATES
OF THE UNDEAD

SHORT STORIES OF
ZOMBIES IN THE AMERICAS

BY

VARIOUS AUTHORS

British Library Cataloguing-in-Publication Data
A catalogue record for this book is available from the
British Library

CONTENTS

THE WEDDING GUESTS

W. B. SEABROOK

An elderly and respected Haitian gentleman whose wife was French had a young niece, by name Camille, a fair-skinned octoroon girl whom they introduced and sponsored in Port-au-Prince society, where she became popular, and for whom they hoped to arrange a brilliant marriage.

Her own family, however, was poor; her uncle, it was understood, could scarcely be expected to dower her—he was prosperous, but not wealthy, and had a family of his own—and the French *dot* system prevails in Haiti, so that while the young beaux of the élite crowded to fill her dance-cards, it became gradually evident that none of them had serious intentions.

When she was nearing the age of twenty, Matthieu Toussel, a rich coffee-grower from Morne Hôpital, became a suitor, and presently asked her hand in marriage. He was dark and more man twice her age, but rich, suave, and well educated. The principal house of the Toussel habitation, on the mountainside almost overlooking Port-au-Prince, was not thatched, mud-walled, but a fine wooden bungalow, slate-roofed, with wide verandahs, set in a garden among gay poinsettias, palms and Bougainvillæa vines. He had built a road there, kept his own big motor-car, and was often seen in the fashionable cafés and clubs.

There was an old rumour that he was affiliated in some way with voodoo or sorcery, but such rumours are current concerning almost every Haitian who has acquired power in the mountains, and in the case of men like Toussel are seldom taken seriously. He asked no *dot*, he promised to be generous, both to her and her straitened family, and the family persuaded her into the marriage.

The black planter took his pale girl-bride back with him to the mountain, and for almost a year, it appears, she was not unhappy, or at least gave no signs of it. They still came down to Port-au-Prince, appeared occasionally at the club *soirées*. Toussel permitted her to visit her family whenever she liked, lent her father money, and arranged to send her young brother to a school in France.

But gradually her family, and her friends as well, began to suspect that all was not going so happily up yonder as it seemed. They began to notice that she was nervous in her husband's presence, that she seemed to have acquired a vague, growing dread of him. They wondered if Toussel were ill-treating or neglecting her. The mother sought to gain her daughter's confidence, and the girl gradually opened her heart. No, her husband had never ill-treated her, never a harsh word; he was always kindly and considerate, but there were nights when he seemed strangely preoccupied, and on such nights he would saddle his horse and ride away into the hills, sometimes not returning until after dawn, when he seemed even stranger and more lost in his own thoughts than on the night before. And there was something in the way he sometimes sat staring at her which made her feel that she was in some way connected with those secret thoughts. She was afraid of his thoughts and afraid of him. She knew intuitively, as women know, that no other woman was involved in these nocturnal excursions. She was not jealous. She was in the grip of an unreasoning fear. One morning when she thought he had been away all night in the hills, chancing to look out of a window, so she told her mother, she had seen him emerging from the door of a low frame building in their own big garden, set at some distance from the others and which he had told her was his office where he kept his accounts, his business papers, and the door always locked. . . . 'So, therefore,' said the mother, relieved and reassured, 'what does this all amount to? Business troubles, those secret thoughts of his, probably . . . some coffee combination he is planning and which is perhaps going wrong, so that he sits up all night at his desk figuring and devising, or rides off to sit up half the night consulting with others. Men are like that. It explains itself. The rest of it is nothing but your nervous imagining.'

And this was the last rational talk the mother and daughter ever had. What subsequently occurred up there on the fatal night of the first wedding anniversary they pieced together from the half-lucid intervals of a terrorized, cowering, hysterical creature, who finally went stark, raving mad. But what she had gone through was indelibly stamped on her brain; there were early periods when she seemed quite sane, and the sequential tragedy was gradually evolved.

On the evening of their anniversary Toussel had ridden away, telling her not to sit up for him, and she had assumed that in his preoccupation he had forgotten the date, which hurt her and made her silent. She went away to bed early, and finally fell asleep.

Near midnight she was awakened by her husband, who stood by the bedside, holding a lamp. He must have been some time returned, for he was fully dressed now in formal evening clothes.

'Put on your wedding dress and make yourself beautiful,' he said; 'we are going to a party.' She was sleepy and dazed, but innocently pleased, imagining that a belated recollection of the date had caused him to plan a surprise for her. She supposed he was taking her to a late supper-dance down at the club by the seaside, where people often appeared long after midnight. 'Take your time,' he said, 'and make yourself as beautiful as you can—there is no hurry.'

An hour later when she joined him on the verandah, she said, 'But where is the car?'

'No,' he replied, 'the party is to take place here,' and she noticed that there were lights in the outbuilding, the 'office' across the garden. He gave her no time to question or protest. He seized her arm, led her through the dark garden, and opened the door. The office, if it had ever been one, was transformed into a dining-room, softly lighted with tall candles. There was a big old-fashioned buffet with a mirror and cut-glass bowls, plates of cold meats and salads, bottles of wine and decanters of rum.

In the centre of the room was an elegantly-set table with damask cloth, flowers, glittering silver. Four men, also in evening clothes, but badly fitting, were already seated at this table. There were two vacant chairs at its head and foot. The seated men did not rise when the girl in her bride-clothes entered on her husband's arm. They sat slumped down in their chairs and did not even turn their heads to greet her. There were wine-glasses partly filled before them, and she thought they were already drunk.

As she sat down mechanically in the chair to which Toussel

led her, seating himself facing her, with the four guests ranged between them, two on either side, he said, in an unnatural strained way, the stress increasing as he spoke:

'I beg you . . . to forgive my guests their . . . seeming rudeness. It has been a long time . . . since . . . they have . . . tasted wine . . . sat like this at table . . . with . . . with so fair a hostess. . . . But, ah, presently . . . they will drink with you, yes . . . lift . . . their arms, as and . . . dance with you . . . more . . . they will . . .'

Near her, the black fingers of one silent guest were clutched rigidly around the fragile stem of a wine-glass, tilted, spilling. The horror pent up in her overflowed. She seized a candle, thrust it close to the slumped, bowed face, and saw the man was dead. She was sitting at a banquet table with four propped-up corpses.

Breathless for an instant, then screaming, she leaped to her feet and ran. Toussel reached the door too late to seize her. He was heavy and more than twice her age. She ran still screaming across the dark garden, flashing white among the trees, out through the gate. Youth and utter terror lent wings to her feet, and she escaped. . . .

A procession of early market-women, with their laden baskets and donkeys, winding down the mountainside at dawn, found her lying unconscious far below, at the point where the jungle trail emerged into the road. Her filmy dress was ripped and torn, her little white satin bride-slippers were scuffed and stained, one of the high heels ripped off where she had caught it in a vine and fallen.

They bathed her face to revive her, bundled her on a pack-donkey, walking beside her, holding her. She was only half conscious, incoherent, and they began disputing among themselves as peasants do. Some thought she was a French lady who had been thrown or fallen from a motor-car; others thought she was a *Dominicaine*, which has been synonymous in creole from earliest colonial days with 'fancy prostitute.' None recognized her as Madame Toussel; perhaps none of them had ever seen her. They were discussing and disputing whether to leave her at a hospital of Catholic sisters on the outskirts of the city, which they were approaching, or whether it would be safer—for them—to take her directly to police headquarters and tell their story. Their loud disputing seemed to rouse her; she seemed partially to recover her senses and understand what they were saying. She told them her name, her maiden family name, and begged them to take her to her father's house.

There, put to bed and with doctors summoned, the family were able to gather from the girl's hysterical utterances a partial comprehension of what had happened. They sent up that same day to confront Toussel if they could—to search his habitation. But Toussel was gone, and all the servants were gone except one old man, who said that Toussel was in Santo Domingo. They broke into the so-called office, and found there the table still set for six people, wine spilled on the table-cloth, a bottle overturned, chairs knocked over, the platters of food still untouched on the sideboard, but beyond that they found nothing.

Toussel never returned to Haiti. It is said that he is living now in Cuba. Criminal pursuit was useless. What reasonable hope could they have had of convicting him on the unsupported evidence of a wife of unsound mind?

And there, as it was related to me, the story trailed off to a shrugging of the shoulders, to mysterious inconclusion.

What had this Toussel been planning—what sinister, perhaps criminal necromancy in which his bride was to be the victim or the instrument? What would have happened if she had not escaped?

I asked these questions, but got no convincing explanation or even theory in reply. There are tales of rather ghastly abominations, unprintable, practised by certain sorcerers who claim to raise the dead, but so far as I know they are only tales. And as for what actually did happen that night, credibility depends on the evidence of a demented girl.

So what is left?

What is left may be stated in a single sentence:

Matthieu Toussel arranged a wedding anniversary supper for his bride at which six plates were laid, and when she looked into the faces of his four other guests, she went mad.

THE ZOMBIE OF ALTO PARANA

W. Stanley Moss

From his deck-chair on the veranda, Emil could see the paddle-boat nosing around the bend in the river. Like a water beetle it came, squat and ungainly, insinuating its crustacean frame with a fanfare of hooting and splashing into the placid exhalations of the landscape.

Once a month the boat from Buenos Aires came up the Alto Parana to the Jesuit country of Misiones, and always it stopped alongside the tongue of land where Emil's bungalow squatted at the water's edge. When, as now, the river was low, a fringe of beach would separate the water from the curtain of *tacuara* which rose to the height of the jungle behind; but later, when the rains began, the beach would vanish overnight, and Emil would awaken to find the water lapping at the wooden stays which supported the veranda on which he slept.

The boat never stayed at the station for more than an hour, but remained just so long as the business of unloading, the checking of inventories and the signing of receipts took to be concluded. And now Emil watched the ungainly craft looming larger before him, its paddles churning up a trail of muddy water which receded like some monstrous reptile in its wake. He saw Silvestro, the foreman, and a couple of Indians making their way along the wooden jetty so as to be ready to start unloading. These things he viewed with detachment, as though he were the spectator of a film which he had seen many times before. The sight bored him.

A sallow-faced, compact figure, with a straggling red beard and down-slanting eyes and little hair on top of his head, he looked like one of those portraits which present an altogether different picture when you turn them upside down. If you had inverted his face, you would have seen an unshaven Chinaman wearing a large red fur hat.

Presently he got up and sauntered down to the water's edge.

Sitting in the captain's cabin, papers before him on the desk and a glass of warm whisky in his hand, he looked up and said: 'That's the lot signed. Is there anything else?'

The captain was an elderly man. Hair grew in abundance from his nostrils and ears. His clothes were shabby, and the glossy peak of his cap was cracked in half. 'There's one more thing,' he replied. 'I've got a passenger on board who wants to get off here.'

'Get off here? What on earth for?'

'He wanted to go as far as the boat would take him.'

'Why?'

'Don't get me wrong. I didn't ask him to come. He paid his fare and I brought him, that's all.'

'What does he want?'

'He's going to make his fortune,' the captain said. 'It's the same old story. But he seems quite a nice young fellow. Couldn't you put him up for a while?'

'You know very well that I refuse to have anybody staying with me.'

The captain had eyes of pale, tired blue – blue that grows thinner and more delicate with the years – and he glanced at Emil, eyebrows raised. 'Are you still adamant?' he asked, and then, when he saw that the other did not intend to answer him, 'What about the hut?' he added. 'The hut on the point? It's been empty since Schlesinger died, hasn't it?'

'Yes,' said Emil, as though caught off guard, 'yes, it's empty. I suppose he could stay there if he wanted to.'

He turned his back on the captain and poured himself another glass of whisky from the decanter on the filing cabinet. He was thinking of Schlesinger, the last mad night, and having to carry the still-warm body two hundred yards through the rain and dumping it in the river. 'But I'm against it. I know what happens when two people get stuck in a place like this.'

'Like you and Schlesinger?' the captain suggested.

'Yes. Like me and Schlesinger.'

The captain spread out his hands on the desk. 'Don't be cruel to this boy,' he said, now raising his right hand as if in absolution. 'He's not like Schlesinger.'

Emil wheeled around, the whisky splashing out of his glass, his hand trembling. 'Stop acting, you old quack!' he snapped. 'Don't you start preaching at me.' He came close to the desk and gripped its edges, and leaned across it so that his beard fell almost in the captain's face. In his down-slanting eyes there gleamed a veneer of power, the knowledge that his shaft had struck on tender skin. 'You know as well as I do that everybody turns into a Schlesinger here, no matter how they start.'

And then the door opened, and they looked up and saw the young man standing in the entrance. He was wearing an open-necked shirt and shorts, and on his bare knees the skin had gone lobster-red with sunburn. His blond hair, his peeling nose and wide-open expression gave him the appearance of a schoolboy who has just had a wash and comes to present himself at the tea-table. When he saw Emil he stopped, his hand still on the door-knob, and hesitantly he said: 'I – I'm most awfully sorry. Am I interrupting something?'

The captain's sigh of relief was audible. 'No,' he quickly replied, his blue eyes creasing in tune with the smile that crept upon his lips. 'Not at all. We've finished our business.' Then he rose from his chair and said: 'I'd like you to meet one another. Emil, this is Mr Clift whom I've brought along from BA.'

'That's right,' said the young man, his countenance brightening. 'We've had a splendid trip, absolutely thrilling. I'm almost sorry it's come to an end, really. But the skipper's told me lots about you and I know that it'll be grand here. I'm terribly glad to meet you.' He spoke very quickly, erratically, as though he had a lot to say and all too little time in which to say it. Now he forsook his place in the doorway and came forward, blushing slightly beneath the lobster over-coating of his skin, and made as if to shake Emil by the hand.

For a moment Emil watched his approach, making no move to accept the proffered hand, then turned abruptly to the captain. 'Is there anything else?' he asked, his lips curling in a sneer. 'Anything else, Father?'

'I hope you'll show Mr Clift the ropes a bit. And perhaps you could let him have a bed in your bungalow until Schlesinger's hut is ready. . . .'

Emil made no reply. Behind him, he heard Clift saying: 'That really would be terribly decent of you.'

They left the jetty and started to walk towards the bungalow. Emil noticed the expression on the young man's face, the rather incredulous look in his eyes as he saw the building for the first time. There was no concealment of his thoughts, and Emil understood them. He remembered how he himself had experienced that same feeling when first he had set eyes upon this pile of wood and corrugated iron. 'So this is my home,' he had thought, a ripple of disgust trembling down his spine.

'So this is your home,' Clift said.

'That's right. Don't you find it charming?'

As if in reply there came a hoot from the boat's siren, and turning they saw the paddles beginning to churn in reverse as the craft put off from the jetty and swung away into the centre of the river.

'Look,' said Clift. 'The skipper's waving to us.' He started waving his arms in return and shouted a good-bye which was inaudible above the noise of the engines. Then he turned to Emil. 'Isn't he a delightful old man – the skipper, I mean? Such an unusual type for this part of the world. I always imagined that the captains of river-boats were hard-drinking, cursing, tobacco-spitting tyrants; but not a bit of it. Just the reverse, in fact. He's so gentle and quiet – more like a priest, really.'

'Emil grunted. 'He *was* a priest – once upon a time – the old fool.'

'You mean?'

'No, he wasn't defrocked. He just gave it up because he

hadn't got the guts to go on with it. But that was years ago, before you were born.'

And then, before the other had time to reply, Emil waved to the foreman on the jetty. 'Silvestro!' he called. 'Come here!' The foreman came running up the stretch of sand to where they stood. He was an elderly man, tight-skinned, with a small head which looked like an Aztec skull that had been arrested in its shrinkage.

'Silvestro, I want you to have Mr Clift's things taken to my bungalow for tonight. He'll stay in the spare room until you've got Schlesinger's hut ready.' To Clift, Emil said: 'This is Silvestro, my *capataz*. He'll be able to help you if you need anything.'

'Thank you,' said Clift. 'Thank you very much.' He did not face Emil as he spoke. He was looking away along the river, watching the boat as it straightened out in midstream and started with a hustle of paddles to churn its way out of sight. He heard Emil saying, 'Come on, I'll show you your room,' but he found himself unwilling to take his eyes from the boat. Again he was the schoolboy, reluctant to leave the carriage window while he could still see his parents waving good-bye to him from the platform; but then he slowly turned and found himself looking once more towards the bungalow – the school, first night away from home, nostalgia and a pillow wet with tears.

Still Emil was talking. 'Good chap, Silvestro. He's a sort of magician at producing things. He'll be able to fix you up with a *compañera* if you want one.' He glanced at the young man. 'I suppose you *do* want one?'

'A *compañera?* I don't know what that means.'

Emil chuckled into his beard. 'Child,' he said. 'It's a sort of wife which can cook.'

'You mean an Indian girl?'

'What did you expect, a white one?'

'No, but – '

'They are quite cheap, and you can change them if you don't find them satisfactory.'

'I – I don't think I really need one.'

Emil laughed out loud; then suddenly he stopped and said: 'Now I'll take you to your room.'

Clift was glad. 'Grand,' he said, with eagerness pursuing the change of subject. 'There must be a splendid view of the river from the bungalow.'

They did not meet again until dusk.

Emil was lying on his bed when he heard a knock on the door and Clift's voice asking: 'May I come in?'

'What do you want?'

'I wondered if you could lend me a mirror?'

'Come in, come in. There's no need to shout.'

Clift entered, a hand stuffed shyly in his pocket, and

stood just inside the doorway. 'I've just been unpacking,' he explained, 'and I found my mirror smashed to smithereens.' He laughed nervously. 'Seven years' bad luck, I suppose.' Then, after a pause, added: 'Do you think you could lend me yours?'

'Mine?' Emil grunted and sat up so that his legs dangled over the edge of the bed. 'What makes you think I've got a mirror?'

'Well – after all – one likes to look fairly presentable. . .'

'For whose benefit? Mine?' Emil burst out laughing, the wind whistling through his teeth and his red beard twitching. 'Presentable!' he echoed. 'That's wonderful!'

Clift stood with his back against the door, his fingers jingling a bunch of keys in his pocket. 'I don't see what's so funny about it,' he said, abashed.

'You'll see what's funny all right,' Emil told him. 'You'll find out in time. Shall I tell you something? I broke my mirror too. I can't remember now how long ago that was . . . perhaps it was seven years ago, perhaps it was yesterday. But do you know how I broke it? Can you guess? No? Well, I'll tell you. I put my fist through it, bang in the middle, because I couldn't stand the sight of it any longer.'

They had supper on the veranda, and afterwards, with cigars and drinks, settled themselves in deck-chairs overlooking the river. From here they could see the red eyes of the alligators, like coupled tail-lamps straying across the water, while to their ears there came the first notes, the tuning-up, of the frog orchestra.

'Do you hear the noise of frogs? It sounds crazy, doesn't it? But it isn't creepy, not eerie like the *uru-tau*. You wait until you hear the *uru-tau*. It's unearthly. Sends the shivers down your back.'

Clift asked: 'What is it? An animal or something?'

'It's a night-bird. The Indians say it contains the souls of haunted men. I'm inclined to believe them. It laughs like a madman, like a raving lunatic. You'll understand when you hear it.'

Emil stretched a hand for the bottle of *caña* beneath his chair and refilled his glass, then: 'It was one of the things that really got Schlesinger,' he continued. 'That, and the red eyes of the alligators. He got so he used to see alligators everywhere.' He held out the *caña* bottle towards Clift. 'Help yourself to another drink.'

The other shook his head, and with a flavour of apology he replied: 'Thanks very much, but I don't think I will. I haven't got much taste for that stuff.'

Emil replaced the bottle on the floor. 'You'll soon get used to it,' he said.

Clift made no reply. Instead, 'Who was Schlesinger?' he asked.

'He was the chap who died in the hut which you're going to stay in.'

'He *died* there? What a horrible thought.'

'It was as well that he died.'

'Why? What was wrong with him?'

'There was almost nothing right with him. He lost his reason, he was diseased, he wouldn't eat. But, to tell you the truth, it was rather fascinating to watch his progress. One felt as though one were actually witnessing a metamorphosis. I was quite young then, you know, and I found it strangely amusing. Can you understand that?'

'I – I don't know. I don't think I can. Perhaps you could have done something to help him. . . .'

'There was nothing to be done. He was always drunk, crazy drunk.'

'And what happened to him in the end? What did he die of?'

'The Indians got him, just like that.'

For a while Clift said nothing; then he gave a nervous little laugh and said: 'Well, that won't happen to me, thank goodness. I'm not staying here long enough – just a matter of days while I find a good guide and collect the necessary kit.'

'And where do you think you're going?'

'Into the jungle. I heard there was silver to be found in

the hills.'

'Who told you so?'

'There've already been one or two expeditions, haven't there?'

'Certainly. But who's to know if they ever found anything? They never came back.' Emil paused for a moment to sip his drink. 'Do you realise that you have to cut your way through every yard of this jungle? It could take you a week to travel a quarter of a mile.'

'I've been told that it's going to be very difficult, but I'm determined to have a try. I've got to make money, lots of it.' He clasped his hands across his knees, and, as if in a nutshell to explain the reason for his expedition, added: 'You see, I've got a debt to pay.'

'A debt? Do you mean to say that you're proposing to go and get buried in there' – Emil waved a hand airily towards the jungle that lay behind the bungalow – 'buried alive just because of a debt? Well, I'm damned! That's the sort of crazy thing one would expect to hear from an Englishman.' Then, as if the thought had not until that moment struck him, he asked: 'I suppose you *are* English, aren't you?'

'Of course. Didn't you know?'

'You never told me.'

'By my accent, I mean.' Clift turned towards his companion. 'I'm sorry,' he said. 'It never struck me that you might not have guessed I was English – any more than I could have doubted that you were a German.'

'Did you say German?'

Emil spoke the words very slowly, as though to chew each one before spitting it out. 'What makes you think I'm a German?'

'I – I really don't know. Just instinct, I suppose. You look like a German, and you talk like one.'

Emil said: 'If ever you repeat those words in front of the Indians, I'll wring your neck.' And then he burst into a great roar of laughter, drowning Clift's attempted apology, and slapped his thigh with barrack-room gusto. 'Go on,' he urged, the mirth still bubbling within him. 'What debt do you owe? Tell me all about it.'

The Englishman, reluctant to reply, drew into himself like some pricked mollusc.

Emil patted him on the knee. 'Don't be silly,' he said. 'I've got to be humoured. I've been here for a long time, you know, and I'm not much accustomed to company.'

Clift's rosy face looked sulky. 'It's a debt of honour. I can't go back to England until I'm in a position to clear it.' He clasped his hands together, as if to crush some invisible nut between his palms. 'It's as simple as that.'

'Simple, my foot! It's mad, crazy. My dear fellow, if it's only money you want – '

'*Only* money?' Clift interrupted, eyebrows up, hands raised. 'For what else could one want to come to a place like this? Surely you don't stay here for pleasure?'

'There are other things,' said Emil. 'If it was only money that I wanted I could have retired years ago. Why, you could make a fortune here even by selling *caña* to the Indians.'

'But that's illegal, isn't it?'

'Everything's illegal. But who's to stop you up here?'

'Things like that get known.'

'You think so? Why don't you try it and see?'

'I've got my plans. I believe that everything will turn out all right – my way.' The Englishman yawned loudly, exaggeratedly. 'I feel dog tired. Would you think it rude if I were to turn in now?'

'Am I so forbidding a companion?'

Again the nervous little laugh. 'Of course not. It's just that I'm tired. Didn't get any sleep last night.'

Clift got up from his chair and rested his hands on the balustrade and stood for a moment looking out across the river; then slowly he turned and started to walk towards the door of his bedroom. Emil watched him closely. He knew what the Englishman was feeling. It had been the same that first night with Schlesinger.

From his bedroom door, Clift said, 'Good night, Emil...'

Emil said nothing, but poured himself another glass of

caña. Without turning, he knew that the Englishman had not yet gone into his room, but was still hovering at the door.

'You – you don't mind my calling you by your Christian name, do you? It's more friendly, somehow, especially as we're the only two white men here. . . .'

Emil said: 'For God's sake stop talking like a dying schoolgirl. Good night.'

For a moment there was silence, then he heard the door creak shut behind him; and then, as if in applause, there sounded the full-blooded roar of the frogs' chorus, while from somewhere, not far off in the jungle, there came the mad, chilling laugh of an *uru-tau.*

High above the *tacuara* there rode a round moon, and in the water, flashing, its image dodged like an uncatchable ball among the red eyes of the alligators.

On the eve of Clift's departure into the jungle Emil walked across from his bungalow to Schlesinger's hut and found the Englishman giving his stores a last-minute check-over on the veranda.

'Hullo,' said Clift brightly, looking up from a rucksack's contents which he had emptied out on the veranda floor. He appeared to be in high spirits, as though packing his tuck-box on the last day of term. The ruddiness of his skin had toned down during the past two weeks, but apart from this his appearance was as spruce and as boyish as it had been on the day of his arrival. 'All set, as you can see,' he announced.

The Englishman was smiling. 'I've collected three Guarani porters, and Silvestro has produced a guide for me who says he knows of a good track through the jungle. So everything's shipshape at last. I can scarcely wait to leave.'

'There is no such thing as a track through the jungle. No such thing exists.' Emil glanced at the Englishman's face: the blue eyes, the wavy blond hair, and the chin which was shaved perhaps every third day. There was nothing new in this sight. He had seen it all before – how many years ago? It was as though he were looking at his own ghost; and the realisation sent a chill wind through his bones. For a moment he hesitated, staring before him; then, muttering something beneath his breath, he suddenly turned and started to walk away from the hut.

'What was that you said?' called Clift; but he received no reply.

Clift had gone, and once more life for Emil resumed its normal course. It was not that the Englishman's presence had in any way altered his routine; but the mere existence of another European in the vicinity had created an undercurrent of interest and curiosity; and now that the young man had departed, Emil was conscious of a new emptiness in his life.

It was on a Sunday that Clift had gone, and it was on a Sunday, exactly five weeks later, that he returned.

The sun was low in the sky when Silvestro, the foreman, came running to Emil's bungalow, and Emil, who did not like being disturbed at this time of the day, asked gruffly: 'What's the matter?'

'The Englisher,' panted the foreman. 'He come back, señor.'

Emil was surprised. Curtly he dismissed his *compañera* and came out on to the veranda.

'There,' said Silvestro, 'there, señor.'

Emil followed the foreman's pointing arm until his eyes rested upon a small, lurching figure coming along the narrow fringe of sand between the *tacuara* and the water's edge.

'Shall I go help, señor?' Silvestro asked, already making as if to go; but Emil laid a hand on his arm.

'No, no,' he said. 'He'll be here in about ten minutes. There's nothing you can do to help.'

When Clift arrived he did not go straight to the bungalow, but went instead to Schlesinger's hut, and it was not until supper-time that he came to see Emil. His skin was the colour of walnut stain, and over his chin and upper lip there straggled a film of hairs as though his flesh had gone mouldy. Thus he stood in front of Emil's deck-chair, a look of mingled reticence and embarrassment in his eyes, and said: 'Well, here I am. May I invite myself to supper?'

Emil motioned him to sit down.

'Sorry I couldn't make myself a little more beautiful. I've lost all my kit. Haven't even got any soap, but perhaps – '

'What happened?'

Clift sat down in the empty chair beside Emil, and helped himself to a drink from the bottle of *caña* which stood on the floor. He took a long gulp at the drink, drew the back of his hand across his lips, then said: 'The Indians ran away one night and pinched all the stores. Fortunately, I had a knife and compass in my belt. I realised that it would be hopeless to try to continue alone, so I struck a course for the river. It took me seventeen days to reach it, and another two to make my way back here.'

Emil grunted. 'I could have told you all that before you set off, you pig-headed ass.'

Clift said: 'It's better to find out these things for oneself, otherwise one would never learn anything.'

'Damned silly way of going about it.'

'I don't think so. I know now, for instance, that a human being can live for nineteen days on nothing but slugs and not feel too bad about it. And I've learned another thing. I know that I'll never go on another expedition like that as long as I live.'

Emil looked up, smiling.

The Englishman leaned towards him. 'I know what you're thinking,' he challenged. 'You're thinking that this is the best joke you've heard in ages, aren't you?'

Emil did not reply.

'Well, I'll tell you something. *I* think it's the best joke I've ever heard in all my life.'

During supper Clift talked a great deal and ate very little. 'Funny,' he said, explaining himself, 'I imagined that I'd be able to eat a horse when I got back, but now that all this food is here in front of me I find it somehow nauseating.'

Emil listened to him, fascinated.

The Englishman was sitting with a bottle of *caña* in front of him, and from time to time, without prompting from his companion, he picked it up and refilled his glass. 'Strange thing about the jungle,' he continued, 'is that you don't get frightened by it. You can get into a panic, yes, and perhaps lose your head, but not in the way that you read about in books. You are scared at the very beginning – that's true – but it only lasts so long as you don't find out the secret. I wonder if *you* know the secret of the jungle?'

Emil said nothing.

'Aha! You don't know. So I'll tell you. The secret is that everything, every living being in the whole of the jungle, is scared stiff. Fear travels through the trees like electricity, and there's so much of it on every side of you that – Bingo! – it just cancels itself out. Two minuses make a plus. Just like that. When everybody is somebody, then nobody is anybody. Who was it made that remark? Can't remember now. But whoever he was he knew what he was talking about. He knew all about the jungle. Take off my hat to him. . . .'

He picked up the bottle from the table, and to draw attention to the fact that it was empty, he turned it upside down and shook it. Then he looked across at Emil. 'I say, you haven't got another bottle tucked away somewhere, have you? What about a night-cap?'

Presently they went out on to the veranda and sat down in the deck-chairs overlooking the river.

'I bet you can't guess what I was thinking about most of the time on my way back here? I'll tell you – I was thinking of that idea of yours – the one about selling *caña* to the Indians – and I decided that it wasn't at all a bad proposition. I've got some gold left – had it hidden in my belt – better invest it before it all goes.' He leaned forward with a conspiratorial air. 'Is it really as easy as you said? What are the snags? Will you tell me more about it?'

'There are no snags,' Emil replied. 'The only people you've got to be careful of are the Indians themselves.'

'Of the Indians? Why on earth?'

'Because alcohol makes them behave in a very odd way. You will sell them a bottle of *caña* – a bottle which you have

bought for thirty centavos on the other side of the river –
and you will ask two pesos for it. That's nearly six hundred
per cent profit. OK. In an hour or two perhaps they will
come back and ask you to sell them another bottle. All right,
you sell them the second bottle for five pesos. That's nearly
sixteen hundred per cent profit. . . .'

'And so on? But it sounds too easy for words.'

'That's where you are wrong. It's just the damned-fool
sort of way a person like you would go and land himself in
trouble.'

'Perhaps you'd explain. . . .'

'Rather than sell a third bottle to an Indian you'd do better
to jump off a precipice. Listen, the man is already drunk. He
probably hasn't got the money and knows you are swindling
him. Perhaps he can even see the third bottle hidden under
your bed, and the only thing that's stopping him from having
it is you yourself. For him it's simple arithmetic. You must be
subtracted – that's all.'

'Oh, well, so long as one remembers when to stop it's all
right. Still make a roaring profit. . . .'

Near at hand there sounded the wild laugh of an *uru-tau*,
high pitched at first, then hilariously descending until finally
it died away.

'How I hate that noise. The bloody bird's always laughing
at you, never *with* you. Gets on my nerves. . . .'

One morning during the following week Emil met the Englishman walking along the fringe of sand by the *tacuara*.

'Good morning,' said Clift jauntily. He was unshaven, but the dirtiness of his face was offset by the lively, almost gay blue of his eyes. 'How's life?'

'All right,' Emil told him.

'What about coming to my place for a drink? You haven't seen the hut since I tidied it up. It's looking quite attractive now.'

Emil hesitated. He had once told himself that never again would he set foot in Schlesinger's hut, never, never; but now his resolution gave way to curiosity. 'Why not?' he said, shrugging his shoulders and joining step with the Englishman.

The hut was a two-roomed affair, low on the ground and almost without windows, surrounded on all sides by a corridor-like veranda. 'Not very beautiful from the outside,' said Clift, 'but there's nothing to be done about that.' He led the way up the steps on to the veranda and threw wide one of the doors that led off it. 'Need a few chintzes, I suppose, and some geraniums. Good old cottagey atmosphere. For geraniums read orchids throughout – exotic note.'

Emil stood in the open doorway looking around the bedroom. He saw a large, brand-new mirror hanging over the wash-basin in the corner, while partly concealed beneath the bed he noticed a cluster of long-necked bottles. Clift followed the direction of his eyes. 'Business is booming,' he said, his voice undergoing an inflexion of cheerfulness. 'Sold a couple of dozen yesterday. Managed to swap one for that mirror, too. Jolly nice mirror, isn't it?' He walked across to the washstand and regarded his reflection in the glass. 'Got to be able to keep an eye on my beard, you know. It's coming on, don't you think? Not as good as yours yet, but just wait and see.' He stroked his chin, fondling the flimsy growth which straggled across his skin. Over his shoulder he asked: 'Like a drink?'

'Not now.'

'Mind if I have one?' He moved away from the mirror and pulled one of the bottles from under his bed. As he uncorked it he said: 'Had a spot of bother last night. One chap wanted to buy a third bottle – just like you said – and we had a bit of a row. It was nothing very serious, but I beat him up just to show him who's wearing the trousers around here. Don't suppose there'll be any more trouble now.' He swallowed a mouthful of *caña* straight from the bottle and wiped his hand across his lips. 'Incidentally, do you remember asking me if I needed a *compañera*? You know, a sort of cook extraordinary? Well, I've been thinking that perhaps it wouldn't be a bad idea after all.'

Once the rains started the visits of the paddle-boat became less regular, and the captain, so as not to risk injury to his craft, was in the habit of travelling only by daylight and mooring for the night at any station where dusk had found him. So it was that one evening the boat drew up alongside the jetty, and from his veranda Emil could hear the captain shouting orders that the boat should be made fast to its moorings for the night. The rain was coming down hard, and already it was too late to start unloading, so Emil sent Silvestro with a message to the captain asking him if he would care to come and have some dinner on shore.

At seven o'clock the captain arrived. He was extremely grateful, he said, for the invitation. He hadn't seen Emil in such good spirits or in so kindly a frame of mind since – well, since the old days when Schlesinger had been alive.

'You know, Emil,' he said, as they sat taking a drink before supper, 'it never did you any good to live here absolutely alone. You are a person who needs company. It's natural for a fellow to become morose and depressed if he doesn't see another civilised being for months on end. Why, you're a changed man now that you've got a companion again.' The older man was nodding, the wrinkles around his eyes creasing into a smile of satisfaction. 'How is he, by the way?'

Emil said: 'I think he's all right. But I don't see a great deal of him, you know.'

'And what does he do with himself?'

'A bit of trading.'

'Successful? He was so keen to make a lot of money when he came out. Something about a debt in England. He told me about it on the way here.'

Emil laughed. 'I don't think his intentions are quite so honourable now.'

The captain was surprised. 'Really?' he queried. 'He seemed so earnest, so determined at the time. Isn't it extraordinary how quickly people can change out here? Why, it isn't even a year since he came to this place, is it?'

'Eight or nine months, that's all. But it feels like a long time.'

The captain said: 'I'd quite like to see him. He seemed such a nice young fellow. I suppose he's coming over for supper?'

'For supper? No, I don't think he'll come. As a matter of fact, I didn't think of asking him. We never eat together.'

'You *never* eat together? But how extraordinary! I simply don't understand. . . .'

'You wouldn't,' said Emil.

'But – but is there something wrong? Anything the matter with him?'

'Voluntary liquidation, that's all. He's got a *compañera* now, and lots of *caña*. I think he's quite happy – after a fashion. We leave each other alone.'

'I see,' muttered the old captain, touching together the tips of his fingers in one of his more priestly attitudes. 'But I can scarcely believe it. What's wrong with him? DTs?'

'Worse than Schlesinger,' said Emil.

Not until supper was over did the captain return once more to the subject of Clift. He broached it tentatively, uncertain what would be his companion's reaction to its repetition. 'You know, Emil,' he said, 'it's about this fellow, Clift. I can't get over what you told me about him. It seems all wrong somehow. Please don't think I'm trying to interfere or anything, but –'

'There's nothing to be done.'

The captain's voice verged on timidity. 'Are you sure about that?' he asked. 'After all, eight months isn't a very long time. . . .'

'It's long enough.'

'I know you'll laugh at me. But I was wondering if you wouldn't take me to see him. . . .'

Emil said: 'By all means go, if you want to. But I think you'll find it's a waste of time.'

With a flash-lamp to guide them, they walked through the rain along the higher path which followed the fringe of *tacuara* towards Schlesinger's hut. When first they came to the clearing at the end of the path they were unable to discern the outline of the hut, for there was no light burning in any window; and it was only because they could hear the resonant humming of rain upon the corrugated-iron roof that they knew they had reached it.

'Wonder where he is?' muttered the captain.

Then like a fist, a loud voice checked them.

'Who's there?'

Emil stopped. He did not flash the torch in the direction of the voice, but instead lowered the beam and quietly said: 'It's me – Emil.'

'What the hell do you want?'

'We just walked over to see you. The skipper's here. He thought it would be nice if – '

'It's out of visiting hours.'

Now their eyes had grown accustomed to the darkness, and they were able to see him, stark naked, sitting in a wicker chair on the veranda, his legs propped up on top of the balustrade.

'Visiting hours,' he went on, 'Mondays and Thursdays, three o'clock.' Then he lowered his legs and leaned forward so that his face came close to the railings. 'Why do you come creeping up like this in the middle of the night? What's the idea of spying on me?'

The captain said: 'You remember me, don't you? We weren't spying. I merely thought that it would be pleasant to call on you and have a chat.'

'Chat about what?'

'About anything you like. I thought maybe you'd want to hear the latest news from Buenos Aires; and besides, I wanted to see how you're getting on out here.'

'Why can't you mind your own business? I suppose you want me to sell you a bottle of plonk. Is that why you came? Well, you can have one. Five pesos. Cash down.'

'May we come in out of the rain?' asked the captain.

'No. You might be shocked. Wouldn't do to shock an old gentleman.' They heard the tinkle of a bottle-neck against the rim of a glass. 'Anyhow, I don't want any haggling. Five pesos – no more, no less.'

'I don't want to buy a bottle,' said the captain.

'Well, what the hell do you want then?'

Emil took the captain by the sleeve. 'Come on,' he said impatiently; but the elder man checked him and said to Clift: 'Why are you sitting in the dark like that?'

'Why?' came the turbid echo. For a moment there was silence, save for the rain on the tin roof and the croaking of frogs in the *tacuara*. Then Clift started to laugh, and once more put his face close to the bars of the balustrade. 'Do you know what you look like from here? You look like a couple of monkeys in the zoo. Very wet and miserable. You'll start sprouting in a minute. If you stand long enough in the rain, you'll go green – just like everything else around here – the sky, the rain, the river, even the mud and the leather of your boots. Horrible colour – too clean, too glib. What wouldn't you give to see red again – lovely sticky bloody red? Red!' Suddenly he threw up his arms and jumped to his feet. 'For God's sake go away!' he shouted. 'Stop standing there and staring like a couple of apes. Go away! Go away and leave me alone!'

An empty bottle splashed into the mud at their feet.

Emil saw the wildly gesticulating body as it pranced across the veranda; and in his ear he heard the hollow voice of the captain saying: 'It's you, Emil, damn you. It's you who have done this.'

Emil was still asleep when the door of his bedroom opened and a stream of sunlight fell across his eyelids. From somewhere a long way off he heard a voice saying, 'Good morning,' and suddenly he found himself wide awake, sitting up in bed and seeing the figure of Clift in the open doorway.

'What the devil do you mean,' he demanded, 'bursting into here at this hour of the morning?' His throat was still thick with sleep, his voice clogged.

'I wanted to be certain of catching you,' replied the Englishman. 'Besides, it isn't as early as all that. I only wanted to ask you one question.'

Emil lit himself a cigarette. 'Well, what is it?'

'I want to know when the next boat's due in again.'

'You know as well as I do that it calls once a month.'

There was embarrassment, almost shyness in the Englishman's face – an expression he had not worn since the first days after his arrival – as he replied: 'Yes, but when did it call last? I don't seem to remember having seen it for quite a long time. My memory's a bit hazy, you know. . . . I haven't been too well lately. . . .'

'Why do you want to know when the boat's coming?'

'Why? Because I want to catch it. I've decided to go back.'

'And is that the reason why you've come and woken me up – just to tell me that?'

'This place is getting me down, Emil. I want to get away from it before – before it's too late.'

'You're crazy.'

'Perhaps – perhaps I am – but not completely. I've suddenly become disgusted by myself. I often used to think that it would be fun to go to pot – you know, chuck everything overboard – but now that I've tried it. . . . It's funny, but I can scarcely remember a thing that has happened during the past year. But a man needs memory. Life is hell without it.'

Emil said: 'You think so? I'd give a great deal to be able to dispense with mine.'

'You are an older man,' Clift replied, then hesitated, uncertain as to how he should qualify his remark. Finally he said: 'I have so little to forget. I often think of what you once told me about that chap Schlesinger; how he became obsessed with small things – the eyes of alligators, a night-bird, the noise of frogs. I can understand him now. All through the rains I found my mental horizon growing narrower and narrower, until finally I was scarcely aware of anything at all. Even the bottles of *caña* just came and went. I suppose I drank most of them, but I can't remember much about it. I might as well have been dead. . . .'

'Why are you telling me all this?' asked Emil.

'Merely to show you that I am independent of you.'

'What do you mean? As far as I'm concerned you could as well not exist.'

'That's not quite true, is it? You're a strange fellow, Emil. I wonder what satisfaction you get out of these – these experiments of yours? I could stay here for another year and you wouldn't care tuppence if you ever saw me or not; but the idea that I might one day decide to go away would be something quite hateful to you.' Now he treated Emil to a smile, as if to wash over the words he had just spoken. 'Well, anyhow, there are no hard feelings so far as I'm concerned. I shall often think of you after I've gone. You've taught me a lot. Perhaps I should even thank you.'

'Oh, shut up,' said Emil. 'I've never heard such drivel in my life.'

On the eve of Clift's departure Emil walked over to the hut and found the Englishman on the veranda, leaning on the balustrade and gazing out across the river.

'Hullo, Emil. I was just taking a look at this view for the last time. The sunset's never been lovelier.'

Clift had shaved off his beard and combed his hair, and except for the colour of his skin, his appearance, at first glance, was as fresh and youthful as on the day of his arrival at the station. It was only upon closer scrutiny that his eyes appeared to lie deeper in their sockets, his lips to be slightly down-turned at the corners, his skin to be drawn more tightly across the framework of bone beneath it.

Emil said: 'I thought we might have a farewell drink together, so I brought this along with me.' From within his shirt he fished out a bottle of whisky. 'Scotch,' he announced, mounting the steps to the veranda and placing the bottle upon the bamboo table in the corner.

'That's terribly nice of you,' said Clift. 'I know how hard it is to come by a bottle of that stuff. But I'm off it, you know. On the wagon. Haven't had a drop for a couple of weeks.'

Emil smiled. 'So Silvestro told me – but I didn't believe it.' He shrugged his shoulders, and over his face, in place of the frozen smile, there crept a look of disappointment. 'Ah, well,' he said, 'it was just an idea. I suppose I shall have to drink it by myself.'

For a moment Clift hesitated, then, 'I'm awfully sorry,' he said. 'I didn't mean to be unsociable. Of course, let's have a drink together – for old times' sake.' And giggling, he added: 'But just one – no more – because I know I'd get terribly tiddly. Funny how quickly one becomes lightheaded once the stuff has gone out of one's system. . . .'

It was dark by the time they finished the bottle, and already the night's voices, like a jazz band which has not yet warmed up, were producing their passionless overture.

Clift said: 'I'm feeling pretty fine.' He tapped the whisky bottle and listened to its empty ring. 'Pity it's finished,' he muttered, and got up and went through the door to his bedroom. A moment later he reappeared, a bottle under each arm and a broad grin on his face. 'I was keeping these as a farewell present for Silvestro,' he announced, placing the bottles on the table, 'but I think we might as well drink them, don't you? I can give him something else instead.'

'Of course, of course,' agreed Emil. 'Silly to stop drinking now – now that we both feel so good.'

'Besides, we've really got something to celebrate this time, eh? Think of it, the last night in this damned hole. Can scarcely believe it. Are you jealous of me Emil? Bet you are, whatever you say. . . .'

Emil was pouring out drinks from one of the fresh bottles. 'Jealous?' he said. 'I don't think so. I'm happy for your sake, but I'm not envious of you. Why should I be?'

Clift laughed. 'Liar,' he said, and leaned forward and patted Emil on the knee. 'Poor old Emil, going to be left behind. You'll be so lonely, all by yourself No one to practise on. No more blood-sucking by remote control. Who'll be your guinea-pig when I've gone? What'll you do with yourself in the evenings?' He thought his last remark was very funny, and again started to laugh. Then suddenly he stopped, and sat bolt upright in his chair. 'Listen,' he half-whispered, raising a finger.

From far off, riding on the night, there sounded the mad laugh of an *uru-tau*.

The Englishman was peering out into the darkness as if his eyes could pierce into the depths of the jungle. 'My spiritual mother,' he said, his voice very low. 'Did you hear her calling?'

'You're mad,' Emil exclaimed. 'As mad as Schlesinger.'

Clift chuckled. 'That's what you'd like to think, isn't it? What a kick it would give you! Can't you hear yourself telling people: "The bird got him – the bird and the alligators and *caña* – just like they got poor old Schlesinger?" Isn't that exactly what you'd say? "I warned him," you'd tell them, "but he took no notice. He wouldn't listen to my advice, the young fool. So he went off his head." Think of the satisfaction you'd get out of being able to say that! The omniscient Emil knows all, sees all, hears all. Sole survivor. Clever fellow.'

Emil said nothing. He was aware of a strange numbness in his brain, as though an old photograph were being projected before his eyes and occupying the entire theatre of his mind. This was Schlesinger sitting in the chair before him – a blond Schlesinger with blue eyes and bare knees – speaking dead words, making the ghosts of gestures. The Englishman was talking to him, but he scarcely heard a word that was said. The voice came to him blurred, through a screen of fog.

'Bloodsucker-in-chief. . . . Thought you'd get me drunk tonight, didn't you, so that I'd start on another bout and miss the boat tomorrow? That was why you brought along the bottle of Scotch, wasn't it? Very cunning – I don't think! Did you imagine I was such a fool as to be taken in by that sort of child's trick?' Again he started chuckling, then leaned forward and refilled his glass to the brim. 'I'm going, Emil. I'm going tomorrow and you'd better get used to the idea because nothing that you can do will stop me. I'm drunk now, so I'll tell you this straight: I despise you – you and your diseased brain. It's you who's mad, not me. You're riddled through and through like a worm-eaten cheese – a dirty German cheese – '

Through clenched teeth Emil said: 'I told you once before

that –'

'You've told me a lot of things. So what?'

Emil was staring at the unopened bottle on the table before him. It was only a few inches away from his fingertips, big and heavy, bigger and heavier as he watched it. His hand crept forward; and then of a sudden he had gripped it around the neck so tightly that it seemed his knuckle-bones would burst right through the skin of his fingers.

'So this,' he said, slowly rising to his feet, the bottle like lead in his hand.

Emil was checking over the pile of canvas bales on the jetty when he heard the captain's voice close behind him.

'Emil, I've got some receipts I'd like you to sign in my cabin. Can you spare a moment?'

Emil shrugged his shoulders. 'All right,' he said, and turned and followed the captain across the gang-plank.

In the cabin the captain said, 'Just the usual lot of stuff. Nothing extra this month.' He walked over to the desk and pushed a sheaf of papers on to the blotter.

Emil sat down and took a pen and started signing the receipts. Paraffin, tinned peaches, mosquito nets, atabrin tablets, oil, a case of rum, corned beef, salt, more salt. . . . He scribbled his name automatically at the bottom of each sheet, not troubling to check the items whose delivery he was acknowledging. He knew that the captain would never cheat him – would never cheat anyone, for that matter, through fear of eternal damnation. For a while the scratching of the pen was the only sound to break the silence in the cabin; but presently, in a voice that simulated casualness, the captain said: 'I've just been having a chat with Silvestro. He told me about Clift. It's too bad.'

'Yes, it's too bad,' Emil agreed, still writing, not looking up. The nib made a noise like a rodent's teeth upon wood.

'Is it true?'

'I don't know what Silvestro told you.'

'He said that Clift had intended to catch the boat today.'

Emil went on writing. Speaking to the papers in front of him: 'Yes,' he replied. 'Yes, I believe he did say something about leaving. But he didn't mention when or how. As you know, we didn't see much of each other.'

'But weren't you with him last night, saying good-bye? Silvestro said he heard voices. . . .'

'Not mine. Never went near the hut. But you know how these Indians love gossip.'

'You mean, you didn't see him at all last night?'

'Not after supper. He came over to my bungalow and asked me to sell him a bottle of Scotch. I let him have one. He didn't say what he wanted it for.'

'Didn't he mention that he was intending to leave?'

'Not then, no. Not a word. He told me he had some

Indians waiting for him at the hut. I presumed he was going to sell them the bottle. Anyway, we scarcely spoke. He was pretty drunk.'

'Drunk? Silvestro didn't think he was. . . .'

Slowly, Emil laid down the pen and leaned forward, his elbows resting upon the papers which were strewn across the blotter. 'What are you getting at?' he demanded. 'Is this an inquisition?'

'I couldn't help my curiosity, Emil. The whole thing reminds me so much of Schlesinger. . . .'

'Except that Schlesinger was killed.'

'But what of Clift?'

'He'll live. I'll look after him all right.'

The captain seated himself upon the edge of the desk, his fingers spreading themselves across the warm mahogany border. 'Emil,' he almost implored, 'why don't you let me bring the young fellow on board? I could take him down to Buenos Aires and have him put in a proper hospital.'

Emil raised his hand. 'Out of the question,' he replied. 'He's far too ill to travel. He'd never stand the journey.'

'But what chance has he got here? You've no facilities, no proper medical kit. . . .'

'I've got my knowledge. That's enough. Besides, he's still unconscious. It would be madness to risk moving him.'

'Silvestro says that his head's in a terrible mess. How do

you think it happened?'

Emil grunted. 'The same old story, I suppose. The young fool didn't take my advice. I told him never to sell a third bottle of liquor to the same Indian. He obviously did.'

'But what of his *compañera*? Surely she could have prevented it?'

'He gave her the sack a fortnight ago. There was nobody with him.'

The captain shook his head, helplessly. Then he asked: 'Will you make me a promise, Emil?'

'That depends. What is it?'

'Promise me to do your best for him. Promise to keep him alive.'

Emil looked indignant. 'What the hell else do you think I'd do? Kill him off? Don't be so damned silly. I'll look after him as though he were my own son. I'm fond of him, you know, even though I don't see much of him, and I enjoy his company too. It'll be nice to have him around for a while longer. . . .'

DEAD MEN WORKING IN THE CANE FIELDS

W. B. Seabrook

Pretty mulatto Julie had taken baby Marianne to bed. Constant Polynice and I sat late before the doorway of his *caille*, talking of fire-hags, demons, werewolves, and vampires, while a full moon, rising slowly, flooded his sloping cotton-fields and the dark rolling hills beyond.

Polynice was a Haitian farmer, but he was no common jungle peasant. He lived on the island of La Gonave, where I shall return to him in later stories. He seldom went over to the Haitian mainland, but he knew what was going on in Port-au-Prince, and spoke sometimes of installing a radio. A countryman, half peasant born and bred, he was familiar with every superstition of the mountains and the plain, yet too intelligent to believe them literally true – or at least so I gathered from his talk.

He was interested in helping me toward an understanding of the tangled Haitian folk-lore. It was only by chance that we came presently to a subject which – though I refused for a long time to admit it – lies in a baffling category on the ragged edge of things which are beyond either superstition or reason. He had been telling me of fire-hags who left their skins at home and set the canefields blazing; of the vampire, a woman sometimes living, sometimes dead, who sucked the blood of children and who could be distinguished because her hair always turned an ugly red; of the werewolf – *chauché*, in creole – a man or woman who took the form of some animal, usually a dog, and went killing lambs, young goats, sometimes babies.

All this, I gathered, he considered to be pure superstition, as he told me with tolerant scorn how his friend and neighbour Osmann had one night seen a grey dog slinking with bloody jaws from his sheep-pen, and who, after having shot and exorcised and buried it, was so convinced he had killed a certain girl named Liane who was generally reputed to be a *chauché* that when he met her two days later on the path to Grande Source he believed she was a ghost come back for vengeance, and fled howling.

As Polynice talked on, I reflected that these tales ran closely parallel not only with those of the negroes in Georgia and the Carolinas, but with the medieval folk-lore of white Europe. Werewolves, vampires, and demons were certainly no novelty. But I recalled one creature I had been hearing about in Haiti, which sounded exclusively local – the zombie.

It seemed (or so I had been assured by negroes more credulous than Polynice) that while the zombie came from the grave, it was neither a ghost nor yet a person who had been raised like Lazarus from the dead. The zombie, they say, is a soulless human corpse, still dead, but taken from the grave and endowed by sorcery with a mechanical semblance of life – it is a dead body which is made to walk and act and move as if it were alive. People who have the power to do this go to a fresh grave, dig up the body before it has had time to rot, galvanize it into movement, and then make of it a servant or slave, occasionally for the commission of some crime, more often simply as a drudge around the habitation or the farm, setting it dull heavy tasks, and beating it like a dumb beast if it slackens.

As this was revolving in my mind, I said to Polynice: 'It seems to me that these werewolves and vampires are first cousins to those we have at home, but I have never, except in Haiti, heard of anything like zombies. Let us talk of them for a little while. I wonder if you can tell me something of this zombie superstition. I should like to get at some idea of how it originated.'

My rational friend Polynice was deeply astonished. He leaned over and put his hand in protest on my knee.

'Superstition? But I assure you that this of which you now speak is not a matter of superstition. Alas, these things – and other evil practices connected with the dead – exist. They exist to an extent that you whites do not dream of, though there is evidence everywhere under your eyes.

'Why do you suppose that even the poorest peasants, when they can, bury their dead beneath solid tombs of masonry? Why do they bury them so often in their own yards, close to the doorway? Why, so often, do you see a tomb or grave set close beside a busy road or footpath where people are always passing? It is to assure the poor unhappy dead such protection as we can.

'I will take you in the morning to see the grave of my brother, who was killed in the way you know. It is over there on the little ridge which you can see clearly now in the moonlight, open space all round it, close beside the trail which everybody passes going to and from Grande Source. For four nights we watched there, in the peristyle, Osmann and I, with shotguns – for at that time both my dead brother and I had bitter enemies – until we were sure the body had begun to rot.

'No, my friend, no, no. There are only too many true cases. At this very moment, in the moonlight, there are zombies working on this island, less than two hours' ride from my own habitation. We know about them, but we do not dare to interfere so long as our own dead are left unmolested. If you will ride with me tomorrow night, yes, I will show you dead men working in the canefields. Close even to the cities there are sometimes zombies. Perhaps you have already heard of those that were at Hasco . . .'

'What about Hasco?' I interrupted him, for in the whole of Haiti, Hasco is perhaps the last name anybody would think of connecting with either sorcery or superstition. The word is American-commercial-synthetic, like Nabisco, Delco, Socony. It stands for the Haitian-American Sugar Company – an immense factory plant, dominated by a huge chimney, with clanging machinery, steam whistles, freight cars. It is like a chunk of Hoboken. It lies in the eastern suburbs of Port-au-Prince, and beyond it stretch the canefields of the Cul-de-Sac. Hasco makes rum when the sugar market is off, pays low wages, a shilling or so a day, and gives steady work. It is modern big business, and it sounds it, looks it, smells it.

Such, then, was the incongruous background for the weird tale Constant Polynice now told me.

The spring of 1918 was a big cane season, and the factory, which had its own plantations, offered a bonus on the wages of new workers. Soon heads of families and villages from the mountain and the plain came trailing their ragtag little armies, men, women, children, trooping to the registration bureau and thence into the fields.

One morning an old black headman, Ti Joseph of

Colombier, appeared leading a band of ragged creatures who shuffled along behind him, staring dumbly, like people walking in a daze. As Joseph lined them up for registration, they still stared, vacant-eyed like cattle, and made no reply when asked to give their names.

Joseph said they were ignorant people from the slopes of Morne-au-Diable, a roadless mountain district near the Dominican border, and that they did not understand the creole of the plains. They were frightened, he said, by the din and smoke of the great factory, but under his direction they would work hard in the fields. The farther they were sent away from the factory, from the noise and bustle of the railway yards, the better it would be.

Better, indeed, for these were not living men and women but poor unhappy zombies whom Joseph and his wife Croyance had dragged from their peaceful graves to slave for him in the sun – and if by chance a brother or father of the dead should see and recognise them, Joseph knew that it would mean trouble for him.

So they were assigned to distant fields beyond the crossroads, and camped there, keeping to themselves like any proper family or village group; but in the evening when other little companies, encamped apart as they were, gathered each around its one big common pot of savoury millet or plantains, generously seasoned with dried fish and garlic, Croyance would tend *two* pots upon the fire, for, as everyone knows, the zombies must never be permitted to taste salt or meat. So the food prepared for them was tasteless and unseasoned.

As the zombies toiled day after day dumbly in the sun, Joseph sometimes beat them to make them move faster, but Croyance began to pity the poor dead creatures who should be at rest – and pitied them in the evenings when she dished out their flat, tasteless *bouillie*.

Each Saturday afternoon Joseph went to collect the wages for them all, and what division he made was no concern of Hasco, so long as the work went forward. Sometimes Joseph alone, and sometimes Croyance alone, went to Croix de Bouquet for the Saturday night *bamboche* or the Sunday cockfight, but always one of them remained with the zombies to prepare their food and see that they did not stray away.

Through February this continued, until Fête Dieu approached, with a Saturday-Sunday-Monday holiday for all the workers. Joseph, with his pockets full of money, went to Port-au-Prince and left Croyance behind, cautioning her as usual; and she agreed to remain and tend the zombies, for he promised her that at the Mardi Gras she should visit the city.

But when Sunday morning dawned it was lonely in the fields, and her kind old woman's heart was filled with pity for the zombies, and she thought, 'Perhaps it will cheer them a little to see the gay crowds and the processions at Croix de Bouquet, and since all the Morne-au-Diable people will have gone back to the mountain to celebrate Fête Dieu at home, no one will recognize them, and no harm can come of it.' And it is true that Croyance also wished to see the gay procession.

So she tied a new bright-coloured handkerchief round her head, aroused the zombies from the sleep that was scarcely different from their waking, gave them their morning bowl of cold, unsalted plantains boiled in water, which they ate dumbly uncomplaining, and set out with them for the town, single file, as the country people always walk. Croyance, in her bright kerchief, leading the nine dead men and women behind her, passed the railroad crossing, where she murmured a prayer to Legba, passed the great white-painted wooden Christ, who hung life-sized in the glaring sun, where she stopped to kneel and cross herself – but the poor zombies prayed neither to Papa Legba nor to Brother Jesus, for they were dead bodies walking, without souls or minds.

They followed her to the market square before the church, where hundreds of little thatched, open shelters, used on weekdays for buying and selling, were empty of trade, but crowded here and there by gossiping groups in the grateful shade.

To the shade of one of these market booths, which was still unoccupied, she led the zombies, and they sat like people asleep with their eyes open, staring, but seeing nothing, as the bells in the church began to ring, and the procession came from the priest's house – red-purple robes, golden crucifix held aloft, tinkling bells and swinging incense-pots, followed by little black boys in white lace robes, little black girls in starched white dresses, with shoes and stockings, from the parish school, with coloured ribbons in their kinky hair, a nun beneath a big umbrella leading them.

Croyance knelt with the throng as the procession passed, and wished she might follow it across the square to the church steps, but the zombies just sat and stared, seeing nothing.

When noontime came, women with baskets passed to and fro in the crowd, or sat selling little sweet cakes, figs (which were not figs but sweet bananas), oranges, dried herring, biscuit, casava bread, and *clairin* poured from a bottle at a penny a glass.

As Croyance sat with her savoury dried herring and biscuit baked with salt and soda, and provision of *clairin* in the tin cup by her side, she pitied the zombies who had worked so faithfully for Joseph in the canefields, and who now had nothing, while all the other groups around were feasting, and as she pitied them, a woman passed crying:

'*Tablettes! Tablettes pistaches! T'ois pour dix cobs!*'

Tablettes are a sort of candy made of brown cane sugar (*rapadou*); sometimes with *pistaches*, which in Haiti are peanuts, or with coriander seed. And Croyance thought, 'These *tablettes* are not salted or seasoned, they are sweet, and can do no harm to the zombies just this once.' So she untied the corner of her kerchief, took out a coin, a *gourdon*, the quarter of a *gourde*, and bought some of the *tablettes*, which she broke in halves and divided among the zombies, who began sucking and mumbling them in their mouths. But the baker of the *tablettes* had salted the *pistache* nuts before stirring them into the *rapadou*, and as the zombies tasted the salt, they knew they were dead and made a dreadful outcry and rose and turned their faces toward the mountain.

No one dared to stop them, for they were corpses walking in the sunlight, and they themselves and everyone else knew that they were corpses. And they disappeared toward the mountain.

When later they drew near their own village on the slopes of Morne-au-Diable, these men and women walking single file in the twilight, with no soul leading them or daring to follow, the people of their village, who were also holding *bamboche* in the market-place, saw them drawing closer, recognized among them fathers, brothers, wives, and daughters whom they had buried months before. Most of them knew at once the truth, that these were zombies who had been dragged dead from their graves, but others hoped that a blessed miracle had taken place on this Fête Dieu, and rushed forward to take them in their arms and welcome them.

But the zombies shuffled through the market-place, recognizing neither father nor wife nor mother, and as they turned leftward up the path leading to the graveyard, a woman whose daughter was in the procession of the dead threw herself screaming before the girl's shuffling feet and begged her to stay; but the grave-cold feet of the daughter and the feet of the other dead shuffled over her and onward; and as they approached the graveyard, they began to shuffle faster and rushed among the graves, and each before his own empty grave began clawing at the stones and earth to enter it again; and as their cold hands touched the earth of their own graves, they fell and lay there, rotting carrion.

That night the fathers, sons, and brothers of the zombies, after restoring the bodies to their graves, sent a messenger on muleback down the mountain, who returned next day with the name of Ti Joseph and with a stolen shirt of Ti Joseph's which had been worn next to his skin and was steeped in the grease-sweat of his body.

They collected silver in the village, and went with the name of Ti Joseph and the shirt of Ti Joseph to a *bocor* beyond Trou Caiman, who made a deadly needle *ouanga*, a black bag *ouanga*, pierced all through with pins and needles, filled with dry goat dung, circled with cock's feathers dipped in blood. And in case the needle *ouanga* be slow in working or be rendered weak by Joseph's counter-magic, they sent men down to the plain, who lay in wait patiently for Joseph, and one night hacked off his head with a machete . . .

* * *

When Polynice had finished this recital, I said to him, after a moment of silence, 'You are not a peasant like those of the Cul-de-Sac; you are a reasonable man, or at least it seems to me you are. Now, how much of that story, honestly, do you believe?'

He replied earnestly: 'I did not see these special things, but there were many witnesses, and why should I not believe them when I myself have also seen zombies? When you also have seen them, with their faces and their eyes in which there is no life, you will not only believe in these zombies who should be resting in their graves, you will pity them from the bottom of your heart.'

Before finally taking leave of La Gonave, I did see these 'walking dead men', and I did, in a sense, believe in them and pitied them, indeed, from the bottom of my heart. It was not the next night, though Polynice, true to his promise, rode with me across the Plaine Mapou to the deserted, silent canefields where he had hoped to show me zombies labouring. It was not on any night. It was in broad daylight one afternoon, when we passed that way again, on the lower trail to Picmy. Polynice reinçd in his horse and pointed to a rough, stony, terraced slope – on which four labourers, three men and a woman, were chopping the earth with machetes, among straggling cotton stalks, a hundred yards distant from the trail.

'Wait while I go up there,' he said, excited because a chance had come to fulfil his promise. 'I think it is Lamercie with the zombies. If I wave to you, leave your horse and come.' Starting up the slope, he shouted to the woman, 'It is I, Polynice,' and when he waved later, I followed.

As I clambered up, Polynice was talking to the woman. She had stopped work – a big-boned, hard-faced black girl, who regarded us with surly unfriendliness. My first impression of the three supposed zombies, who continued dumbly to work, was that there was something about them which was unnatural and strange. They were plodding like brutes, like automatons. Without stooping down, I could not fully see their faces, which were bent expressionless over their work. Polynice touched one of them on the shoulder and motioned him to get up. Obediently, like an animal, he slowly stood erect – and what I saw then, coupled with what I had heard previously, or despite it, came as a rather sickening shock. The eyes were the worst. It was not my imagination. They were in truth like the eyes of a dead man, not blind, but staring, unfocused, unseeing. The whole face, for that matter, was bad enough. It was vacant, as if there was nothing behind it. It seemed not only expressionless, but incapable of expression. I had seen so much previously in Haiti that was outside ordinary normal experience that for the flash of a second I had a sickening, almost panicky lapse in which I thought, or rather felt, 'Great God, maybe this stuff is really true, and if it is true, it is rather awful, for it upsets everything.' By 'everything' I meant the natural fixed laws and processes on which all modern human thought and actions are based. Then suddenly I remembered – and my mind seized the memory as a man sinking in water clutches a solid plank – the face of a dog I had once seen in the histological laboratory at Columbia. Its entire front brain had been removed in an experimental operation weeks before; it moved about, it was alive, but its eyes were like the eyes I now saw staring.

I recovered from my mental panic. I reached out and grasped one of the dangling hands. It was calloused, solid, human. Holding it, I said, '*Bonjour, compère.*' The zombie stared without responding. The black wench, Lamercie, who was their keeper, now more sullen than ever, pushed me away – *'Z'affai' nèg pas z'affai' blanc'* (Negroes' affairs are not for whites). But I had seen enough. 'Keeper' was the key to it. 'Keeper' was the word that had leapt naturally into my mind as she protested, and just as naturally the zombies were nothing but poor ordinary demented human beings, idiots, forced to toil in the fields.

It was a good rational explanation, but it is far from being the end of this story. It satisfied me then, and I said as much to Polynice as we went down the slope. At first he did not contradict me, even said doubtfully, 'Perhaps'; but as we reached the horses, before mounting, he stopped and said, 'Look here, I respect your distrust of what you call superstition and your desire to find out the truth, but if what you were saying now were the whole truth, how could it be that over and over again people who have stood by and seen their own relatives buried, have, sometimes soon, sometimes months or years afterwards, found those relatives working as zombies, and have sometimes killed the man who held them in servitude?'

'Polynice,' I said, 'that's just the part of it that I can't believe. The zombies in such cases may have resembled the dead persons, or even been "doubles" – you know what doubles are, how two people resemble each other to a startling degree. But it is a fixed rule of reasoning in my country that we will never accept the possibility of a thing being "supernatural" so long as any natural explanation, even far-fetched, seems adequate.'

'Well,' said he, 'if you spent many years in Haiti, you would find it very hard to fit this reasoning into some of the things you encountered here.'

As I have said, there is more to this story – and I think it is best to tell it very simply.

In all Haiti there is no clearer scientifically trained mind, no sounder pragmatic rationalist, than Dr Antoine Villiers. When I sat with him in his study, surrounded by hundreds of scientific books in French, German, and English, and told him of what I had seen and of my conversations with Polynice, he said:

'My dear sir, I do not believe in miracles nor in supernatural events, and I do not want to shock your Anglo-Saxon intelligence, but this Polynice of yours, with all his superstition, may have been closer to the partial truth than you were. Understand me clearly. I do not believe that anyone has ever been raised literally from the dead – neither Lazarus, nor the daughter of Jairus, nor Jesus Christ himself – yet I am not sure, paradoxical as it may sound, that there is not something frightful, something in the nature of criminal sorcery if you like, in some cases at least, in this matter of zombies. I am by no means sure that some of them who now toil in the fields were not dragged from the actual graves in which they lay in their coffins, buried by their mourning families!'

'It is then something like suspended animation?' I asked.

'I will show you,' he replied, 'a thing which may supply the key to what you are seeking,' and standing on a chair, he pulled down a paper-bound book from a top shelf. It was nothing mysterious or esoteric. It was the current official *Code Pénal* (Criminal Code) of the Republic of Haiti. He thumbed through it and pointed to a paragraph which read:

'Article 249. Also shall be qualified as attempted murder the employment which may be made against any person of substances which, without causing actual death, produce a lethargic coma more or less prolonged. If, after the administering of such substances, the person has been buried, the act shall be considered murder no matter what result follows.'

The strangest and most chimeric story of this type ever related to me in Haiti by Haitians who claimed direct knowledge of its essential truth is the tale of Matthieu Toussel's mad bride, the tale of how her madness came upon her. I shall try to reconstruct it here as it was told to me – as it was dramatized, elaborated, perhaps, in the oft re-telling.

An elderly and respected Haitian gentleman whose wife

was French had a young niece, by name Camille, a fair-skinned octoroon girl whom they introduced and sponsored in Port-au-Prince society, where she became popular, and for whom they hoped to arrange a brilliant marriage.

Her own family, however, was poor; her uncle, it was understood, could scarcely be expected to dower her – he was prosperous, but not wealthy, and had a family of his own – and the French *dot* system prevails in Haiti, so that while the young beaux of the élite crowded to fill her dance-cards, it became gradually evident that none of them had serious intentions.

When she was nearing the age of twenty, Matthieu Toussel, a rich coffee-grower from Morne Hôpital, became a suitor, and presently asked her hand in marriage. He was dark and more than twice her age, but rich, suave, and well-educated. The principal house of the Toussel habitation, on the mountainside almost overlooking Port-au-Prince, was not thatched, mud-walled, but a fine wooden bungalow, slate-roofed, with wide verandahs, set in a garden among gay poinsettias, palms, and Bougainvillaea vines. He had built a road there, kept his own big motorcar, and was often seen in the fashionable cafés and clubs.

There was an old rumour that he was affiliated in some way with Voodoo or sorcery, but such rumours are current concerning almost every Haitian who has acquired power in the mountains, and in the case of men like Toussel are seldom taken seriously. He asked no *dot*, he promised to be generous, both to her and her straitened family, and the family persuaded her into the marriage.

The black planter took his pale girl-bride back with him to the mountain, and for almost a year, it appears, she was not unhappy, or at least gave no signs of it. They still came down to Port-au-Prince, appeared occasionally at the club soirées. Toussel permitted her to visit her family whenever she liked, lent her father money, and arranged to send her young brother to a school in France.

But gradually her family, and her friends as well, began to suspect that all was not going so happily up yonder as it seemed. They began to notice that she was nervous in her husband's presence, that she seemed to have acquired a vague, growing dread of him. They wondered if Toussel were ill-treating or neglecting her. The mother sought to gain her daughter's confidence, and the girl gradually opened her heart. No, her husband had never ill-treated her, never a harsh word; he was always kindly and considerate, but there were nights when he seemed strangely preoccupied, and on such nights he would saddle his horse and ride away into the hills, sometimes not returning until after dawn, when he seemed even stranger and more lost in his own thoughts than on the night before. And there was something in the way he sometimes sat staring at her which made her feel that she was in some way connected with those secret thoughts. She was afraid of his thoughts and afraid of him. She knew intuitively, as women know, that no other woman was involved in these nocturnal excursions. She was not jealous. She was in the grip of an unreasoning fear. One morning, when she thought he had been away all night in the hills, chancing to look out of a window, so she told her mother, she had seen him emerging from the door of a low frame building in their own big garden, set at some distance from the others and which he had told her was his office where he kept his accounts, his business papers, and the door always locked . . . 'So, therefore,' said the mother relieved and reassured, 'what does all this amount to? Business troubles, those secret thoughts of his, probably . . . some coffee combination he is planning and which is perhaps going wrong, so that he sits up all night at his desk figuring and devising, or rides off to sit up half the night consulting with others. Men are like that. It explains itself. The rest of it is nothing but your nervous imagining.'

And this was the last rational talk the mother and daughter ever had. What subsequently occurred up there on the fatal night of their first wedding anniversary they pieced together from the half-lucid intervals of a terrorised, cowering, hysterical creature, who finally went stark, raving mad. But what she had gone through was indelibly stamped on her brain; there were early periods when she seemed quite sane, and the sequential tragedy was gradually evolved.

On the evening of their anniversary Toussel had ridden away, telling her not to sit up for him, and she had assumed that in his preoccupation he had forgotten the date, which hurt her and made her silent. She went away to bed early, and finally fell asleep.

Near midnight she was awakened by her husband, who stood at the bedside, holding a lamp. He must have been some time returned, for he was fully dressed now in formal evening clothes.

'Put on your wedding dress and make yourself beautiful,' he said; 'we are going to a party.' She was sleepy and dazed, but innocently pleased, imagining that a belated recollection of the date had caused him to plan a surprise for her. She supposed he was taking her to a late supper-dance down at the club by the seaside, where people often appeared long after midnight. 'Take your time,' he said, 'and make yourself as beautiful as you can – there is no hurry.'

An hour later when she joined him on the verandah, she said, 'But where is the car?'

'No,' he replied, 'the party is to take place here.' She noticed that there were lights in the outbuilding, the 'office' across the garden. He gave her no time to question or protest. He seized her arm, led her through the dark garden, and opened the door. The office, if it had ever been one, was transformed into a dining room, softly lighted with tall candles. There was a big old-fashioned buffet with a mirror and cut-glass bowls, plates of cold meats and salads, bottles of wine and decanters of rum.

In the centre of the room was an elegantly set table with damask cloth, flowers, glittering silver. Four men, also in evening clothes, but badly fitting, were already seated at this table. There were two vacant chairs at its head and foot. The seated men did not rise when the girl in her bride-clothes entered on her husband's arm. They sat slumped down in their chairs and did not even turn their heads to greet her. There were wine-glasses partly filled before them, and she thought they were already drunk.

As she sat down mechanically in the chair to which Toussel led her, seating himself facing her, with the four guests ranged between them, two on either side, he said, in an unnatural, strained way, the stress increasing as he spoke:

'I beg you . . . to forgive my guests their . . . seeming rudeness. It has been a long time . . . since . . . they have . . . tasted wine . . . sat like this at table . . . with . . . so fair a hostess . . . But, ah, presently . . . they will drink with you, yes . . . lift . . . their arms, as I lift mine . . .

clink glasses with you . . . more . . . they will arise and .
. . dance with you . . . more . . . they will . . .'

Near her, the black fingers of one silent guest were
clutched rigidly around the fragile stem of a wine-glass,
tilted, spilling. The horror pent up in her overflowed. She
seized a candle, thrust it close to the slumped, bowed face,
and saw the man was dead. She was sitting at a banquet table
with four propped-up corpses!

Breathless for an instant, then screaming, she leaped to
her feet and ran. Toussel reached the door too late to seize
her. He was heavy and more than twice her age. She ran still
screaming across the dark garden, flashing white among the
trees, out through the gate. Youth and utter terror lent wings
to her feet, and she escaped . . .

A procession of early market-women, with their laden
baskets and donkeys, winding down the mountainside at
dawn, found her lying unconscious far below, at the point
where the jungle trail emerged into the road. Her flimsy dress
was ripped and torn, her little white satin bride-slippers were
scuffed and stained, one of the high heels ripped off where
she had caught it in a vine and fallen.

They bathed her face to revive her, bundled her on a pack-
donkey, walking beside her, holding her. She was only half-
conscious, incoherent, and they began disputing among

themselves as peasants do. Some thought she was a French lady who had been thrown or fallen from a motor car; others thought she was a *Dominicaine*, which has been synonymous in creole from earliest colonial days with 'fancy prostitute'. None recognised her as Madame Toussel; perhaps none of them had ever seen her. They were discussing and disputing whether to leave her at a hospital of Catholic sisters on the outskirts of the city, which they were approaching, or whether it would be safer – for them – to take her directly to police headquarters and tell their story. Their loud disputing seemed to rouse her; she seemed partially to recover her senses and understand what they were saying. She told them her name, her maiden family name, and begged them to take her to her father's house.

There, put to bed and with doctors summoned, the family were able to gather from the girl's hysterical utterances a partial comprehension of what had happened. They sent up that same day to confront Toussel if they could – to search his habitation. But Toussel was gone, and all the servants were gone except one old man, who said that Toussel was in Santo Domingo. They broke into the so-called office, and found there the table still set for six people, wine spilled on the table-cloth, a bottle overturned, chairs knocked over, the platters of food still untouched on the sideboard, but beyond that they found nothing.

Toussel never returned to Haiti. It is said that he is living now in Cuba. Criminal pursuit was useless. What reasonable hope could they have had of convicting him on the unsupported evidence of a wife of unsound mind?

And there, as it was related to me, the story trailed off to a shrugging of the shoulders, to mysterious inconclusion.

What had this Toussel been planning – what sinister, perhaps criminal necromancy in which his bride was to be the victim or the instrument? What would have happened if she had not escaped?

I asked these questions, but got no convincing explanation or even theory in reply. There are tales of rather ghastly abominations, unprintable, practised by certain sorcerers who claim to raise the dead, but so far as I know they are only tales. And as for what actually did happen that night, credibility depends on the evidence of a demented girl.

So what is left?

What is left may be stated in a single sentence:

Matthieu Toussel arranged a wedding anniversary supper for his bride at which six plates were laid, and when she looked into the faces of his four other guests, she went mad.

SALT IS NOT FOR SLAVES

G. W. Hutter

Several times before I had noticed the old woman. She always squatted on her low stool as far as possible from the other servants, as if her age did not separate her enough from the young, rollicking blacks. Her years were impossible to reckon. She seemed as old as the island; and a definite, tangible part of it. Haiti's mountains and valleys appeared impressed on her face; and the darkness and mystery of history mirrored in her eyes; eyes which were startling in their strength and intensity; eyes which suggested timelessness more than anything I had ever seen – animate or inanimate. They were incredible in her stooped, bent old body.

She sat immovable save for the quick motions of her long, bony fingers as she sliced pineapples or plucked doves and guineas for the hotel dinner. Her hands worked automatically – she did not need her eyes, which were staring ceaselessly up to the heights of the dark green mountains in the distance.

As I gazed out of my glassless window, waiting for the tropic sun to drop low enough to permit the evening plunge in the concrete 'basin' in the rear garden, I heard a commotion and a violent outburst of Creole. 'Tit Jean, terror-stricken, was scrambling away from the old woman as fast as his little legs could carry him. On the ground by the old woman's stool lay several empty salt cellars, their contents strewn over the grass.

Madame appeared just as the old woman was overtaking the cause of her fury. 'Marie!' she shouted imperatively. The old woman turned, slunk back to her stool, picked it up and resumed her work at the end of the garden.

'Tit Jean was sobbing at the foot of the stairs when I descended in my bathrobe. I asked him the trouble.

'Marie, *pas bonne,*' he declared.

When I asked him why Marie was no good, he told me in Creole, broken by sobs, that when he accidentally tripped in passing her stool, she had tried to kill him because a little salt had fallen on her. Yes, that was everything he had done. Her rage was as inexplicable to me as it had been to him, and I gave him the only comfort I knew – a five centime piece. This seemed to make his world rosy once more.

He smiled, motioned me to come behind the door and then, in a voice so low that I was forced to bend my head to his level, he whispered, 'Voodoo!'

He nodded his head meaningly towards the garden. When I laughed, terror leaped into his round eyes. I had heard many stories of Voodoo in Haiti, but I could not connect the trivial incident of a small boy accidentally spilling a bit of table salt with any of them. 'Tit Jean, however, was silent. He would say no more. Voodoo was too real and serious a matter with him to be discussed laughingly with a white man.

I walked past the old woman. She looked through me as if I did not exist.

I entered the small boarded enclosure of the 'basin', stripped off the bathrobe; and the heat of the day was soon forgotten in the invigorating buoyancy of clear mountain water.

As I walked, dripping wet, by the uplifted eyes, I said, '*Bon soir.*'

'*Bon soir, Monsieur,*' she replied. Even though she hardly glanced at me as she spoke and there was little cordiality in her voice, I felt encouraged. At least she was approachable and I might draw her into conversation.

I was still thinking of her after I had dressed and was seated at dinner. 'Tit Jean was not himself as he served me. He could hardly wait for me to empty the spoon of guava jelly on my guinea; he was in such a hurry to leave the single table I occupied in the corner of the porch. The whites of his eyes showed plainly as I smiled at his uneasiness to be away from me and serve the other guests – they would not ask cynical questions about Voodoo.

As I sipped my after-dinner coffee, I glanced up at the black mountains. I imagined I heard the beat of a tom-tom and I remembered old Marie's gaze directed up to these mountains – seeing all and seeing nothing. 'Tit Jean saw me as I looked at the distant hills, and remained in a corner until I had left the table.

A squawk of a loudspeaker drew me into the large park spreading out before the hotel. A radio concert was being given from the local station and the town had assembled before an enormous receiving set placed in the bandstand. The chatter of Creole was completely stilled by the strains of 'Bye, Bye, Blackbird,' and the native favourite, 'Yes, Sir, That's my Baby.'

Standing in a group, their faces beaming with delight, were the servants from the hotel. They were all there, I noticed, except old Marie. Now was a good chance to see the old woman, I thought. Obviously the servants' work was done for the night and I could catch her alone in the garden. I left the spellbound crowd in the park and paused on my way back to the hotel in a café to buy a large bag of tobacco.

Marie was sitting on her stool as I had hoped. Casually I strolled around the garden and stopped beside her.

'Would you care for some tobacco?' I asked in French.

She reached her bony hand for the bag. 'Oui, *Monsieur*.

You are very kind.'

She began to fill the large calabash pipe which had stuck from her apron pocket. I continued my stroll for a few minutes and then sat down on the outside rim of the 'basin' a few yards from her stool.

She was again staring straight ahead at the mountains.

I lit a cigarette and we both smoked silently. A second cigarette – still another, but not a word from her. She remained motionless – staring.

'You like to look at the hills, Marie?' I began awkwardly.

Without turning she said, 'No, *Monsieur*.'

'Then why do you stare at them?' I was determined to get some returns from my tobacco.

She took three long puffs before she replied very slowly, 'It is because I cannot help but stare at my life. That large mountain is my life. It began at the topmost point and it ends at the bottom. From this seat I can see everything by casting my eyes to the top; and today, *Monsieur*, I have not raised them very high.'

'You were born on the mountain?' I prodded her.

'That I do not know – but many years I spent there as a girl. My master's villa was the only one there. That, also, was many years ago.

'My master was rich and powerful and had many slaves. They say he chose the site for his villa because it was the highest point in all Haiti, and from the door of his home he could look down on his lands extending from Port-au-Prince up to the Cape. His lands were so many that he needed hundreds of slaves to till them and gather in the crops. In some years his coffee alone required a fleet of ships to carry it to France. But he had no mercy for his slaves. He drove them hard, and when they could endure it no more they dropped from exhaustion. Then he sent them up to the slave quarters at the villa just like broken-down horses to be patched up for work again.

'I was always there. I was a house servant. When I grew old enough I loved Tresaint. Tresaint was a big, strong, young man, whom his master trusted. He, like me, was there always, and the master made him the overseer of the other slaves. When business called the master away, Tresaint was left in charge of everything. The key to the salt even was left with him.'

'The salt?' I asked wonderingly.

'Yes, the salt. Years before – almost the first thing I remember – the master called us before him, the six men and me, and gave his command about the salt. "Slaves," he said, "You are to be under my roof always. There is one order you must not disobey. You shall eat no salt. You will grow strong. You will suffer no sickness; but let one grain of salt pass your lips and you die." He looked very stern and grim as he said it, and we knew that it was true.

'We did not ask why. The master was to be obeyed, not questioned. We also knew his powers – powers not in slaves and lands – but other and more mysterious ones he had at his command. That is why we put even the thought of salt from our minds, and grew strong and healthy. Sometimes the quarters were filled with a hundred slaves stricken with the fever of the low rice fields, or with their legs swollen the size of large burros, and all around us were dying like flies; but none of us was sick a day.

'Yes,' Marie went on, 'all of the men were strong, but Tresaint was the strongest of the six. When he held me in his arms I felt as if he would break every bone in my body, but I loved him for it.

'No slave in the country was as well-off as Tresaint, but he was not happy. Always the misery of the worn-out slaves oppressed him. The harsh words and treatment he dealt out to them seemed to hurt him as well. He must treat them severely when the master was around, but when he was away on one of his trips the others would know at once through Tresaint's kindly manner.

'Strange rumours came to our ears, brought by incoming slaves. They said there was a man in the north of the island around the Cape who was preaching freedom. He taught that the slaves should rise up and throw off the yoke of the

French. That they were human beings – not animals – and that they themselves should rule their country. This man was a slave himself. His name was Christophe.'

I gasped. Surely that couldn't have been true! Christophe became Emperor Henry of Haiti in 1804. This would make the old woman almost a hundred and fifty years old. It was impossible. Then I looked in Marie's face – a black rock in the moonlight. She seemed centuries older than anything I had ever seen before. She spoke so surely, seemed so certain of what she was saying. I was confused and undecided.

A creaking of shoes at the garden entrance, a babble of Creole and laughter, and the servants were back from the concert. When they saw Marie and me, their talking and laughter stopped. They went quietly to their rooms strewn back of the kitchen along the edge of garden.

The lights in the hotel were flicked out. Everything was quiet. Marie was puffing rhythmically at her pipe.

'And Tresaint – ' I urged her on. 'Was he interested in these tales of Christophe?'

'Yes, he was interested. He was too interested. That was the cause of everything.' Marie spoke earnestly. 'Christophe, he said, was the saviour of Haiti. France, herself, had thrown off the yoke of her kings and now Haiti should throw off the yoke of France. The black man should rule his own country. All of this Tresaint would tell me until I became worried for fear that the master would learn of his trusted overseer's burning thoughts.

'Finally there came a time when the master himself was aroused. Christophe had persuaded scores of slaves on the master's lands near the Cape to leave their fields of bondage and flee to him. This news sent the master into a mighty rage. He left the villa at once to sail to the Cape.

'Before the master's carriage had reached Port-au-Prince a great change had come over the villa. Shouts, singing and laughter filled the house. Tresaint, who had always been lenient when the master was away, now became the master himself and treated the slaves as if they were the master's guests. He opened up the wine cellar and invited them in. He did not give them the *tafia* in the tin mugs which was kept for the slaves but he rolled out a keg of the finest rum. Rum that was many years old; and he served it to them in the villa's finest glasses. They skipped and danced about and dropped ashes from the master's cigars on the marble floors.

'I was frightened but Tresaint would not listen to me. He was encouraging them into complete lawlessness. He left the slaves in the main salon. Bare feet which before had known only the feel of rocks and sod plopped delightedly across smooth marble. Soon he appeared, his huge arms hugging bottles and bottles of champagne. With a blow from a sword snatched down from the wall, he cut off the necks – the wine popping and gurgling to the floor. When every slave had a bottle Tresaint mounted the mahogany table in the hall.

' "Friends," he shouted, "drink to the health of your new masters – yourselves! We shall be slaves no longer. The day of freedom has come. Drink!" He drained the upraised jagged bottle with one long draught and dashed it in a thousand pieces on the floor.

'The glass cut my feet as I ran to him.

' "Tresaint! Tresaint! Listen to me," I begged. "The master will kill you surely when he returns. Stop this foolish wildness before it is too late.' "

'But the idea of freedom was as strong in his head as the fumes of the liquor. He laughed at my fears and pushed me aside.

' "Women are cowards," he announced to the cheering crowd, "but I am a man. I am no longer afraid of anybody – not even the master. Lose all fear and you shall be free. The master put fear into us from the start. You five men who have been with me here know what this key means." He held out the smallest key that dangled on the chain around his neck.

'I was terrified. I knew the key. It was to the chest that was filled with salt! What madness was he up to now?

'He saw the terror on my face and called, "And you too,

Marie! You were placed in the master's power at the same time – all by his command about the salt. We shall eat no salt. Why? Because the master forbade it and we are not to question his command. Bah!"

'He threw the key at my feet.

' "We will show the master's power is gone. Marie, fetch some salt. We will eat it and be forever free."

'I picked up the key and stumbled out of the room, on past the closet that contained the forbidden chest. From the back gallery I dropped the key beside an orange-tree. I hoped this ruse would delay Tresaint in his madness. That in a little while he would come to his senses again when the rum and the wine wore off and would thank me for preventing him carrying out his rash deed.

'I crouched in the corner of the gallery.

' "Marie! Marie!" his voice thundered out from the house but I did not answer.

'In a few minutes he came out to where I was.

' "Where is the key?" he asked.

'I told him I did not know.

' "That doesn't matter. The chest is not so strong that I cannot open it."

'He put his arm around me.

' "You are too timid," he said.

'I returned his embrace with all my strength. I tried to

draw him down on a bench while I pleaded and cajoled with him to stay with me. I pointed out the truth of the master's curse on the salt. I showed him how we had been strong and healthy always just as the master had foretold and that to disobey him would cause our death. If the master's predictions had worked one way they would work the other. But he would not hear me. I called on his love for me but all to no avail. He left me stricken dumb with terror.

'Sounds of blows on wood, a shout of triumph and Tresaint's voice floated out: "Here, my friends, in one hand you have the salt, in the other the wine to wash the curse away."

'A moment of silence as I shivered in the heat of midday and then more shouts. They were dancing around in the marble salon, yelling exultantly.

'How long I remained frozen to my seat I do not know, but gradually there beat into my ears a curious sound. The pattering of bare feet was all I heard; the shouts and singing had disappeared.

'Fearfully I crept into the room. Along the sides of the wall were stretched out the slaves from the quarters, stupefied by drink. In the centre were Tresaint and the five others skipping around with waving arms without uttering a sound. The marble floor was covered with jagged pieces of bottles.

'I stood in amazement looking at their bare feet. They

seemed unaware of the glass, unaware of everything. Great gashes were in their feet. As he lifted his feet ceaselessly across the floor, two of Tresaint's toes dangled like broken palm leaves. The wounds had a strange unnatural appearance. There was no sign of blood.

'Horrified I looked in Tresaint's face. His eyes did not move, his nostrils and mouth gave no sign of breathing. And as I looked I saw his face set in rigidity, the flesh seemed to drop away leaving nothing but cheek bones and eyes. His ribs stood out through the torn shirt – bare.

'I screamed in horror. He was dead! They were all dead! They were corpses treading a fantastic dance of death.

'My screams awoke the drunken slaves from their stupor. Opening their eyes, without rising from the floor, they saw what I had seen. The truth was plain to them. They cried in terror at the dead dancing bodies. They scrambled to their feet and fled out of the house and down the road. The whole mountainside shook with their yells of horror as they raced away. I was left alone with these prancing shells of men.

'For some reason, I do not know what, unless it was for the love I had borne him, I was impelled to touch him who had been so close to me. I reached for his hand as he passed by in his endless mad dance.

'The fingers closed cold around my hand. The two arms pressed me against the body which stopped still. I could hear and feel my own heartbeat – nothing more. It was as if I was being enfolded by the cool marble of the villa.

'He placed a hand over my heart, then quickly on one of the other forms. He turned his unseeing eyes full from my face to the others. Then those eyes, which had been as glassy and dead as the eyes of a fish two days from the bay, mirrored such horror as the world had never seen. From the dead caverns of the throat came a cry. Half shriek and half groan of such force and terror that my blood froze.'

'The others took up the cry. I was mad from horror.'

Marie was living again those dead days. Her body was shaking with emotion. Her voice rose and fell reflecting all the horror of her story.

She arose from her stool, stepping fantastically in the moonlight, to show how that macabre measure was trod by the moving dead in the glass covered marble of the salon.

I was too engrossed to interrupt. She talked on:

'Those shrieks of horror meant that they knew they were dead. It was their spirits crying out – crying to be released from their dead bodies.

'My hand was still held by the lifeless fingers – fingers without blood, but with all the strength of iron bands.

'With one accord the forms rushed through the villa, bounding me along with them. Down the road they tore. My feet did not seem to touch the ground. I felt as if I were being whisked through the air. I screamed at the top of my lungs, but so mighty were their cries that my ears never received a sound coming from my lips.

'Down, down the road we flew. A sight to strike terror into the bravest heart. For miles the screams could be heard and we met nothing on the road but deserted burros. The travellers had heard the fearful noises and the dust that the leaping spirits raised in the afternoon sun had sent them scurrying from the approaching horror, to a safe retreat from the roadside. God, *Monsieur*, it was such a sight that would strike you dead. Six dead men racing and falling down the road, dragging along a woman more gripped by fear and horror than death itself holds. Heads like death; bodies stripped of clothes, the rags fluttering behind them; skeleton ribs showing the dust of the road through their gaunt gaps; the fleshless arms raised, threshing the air; and above all the shrill, deep unearthly yells that came from still throats. On down the road!'

Marie had worked herself up into a fearful pitch of excitement. She arose from her stool.

'Like this they ran!' And with that she threw open her dress, lifted her arms and began bounding around the garden. Her dress trailed after her as she ran, her arms clutched wildly at the air, and from her throat came a low horrible cry.

There in the moonlight I myself saw that mad race down

the mountain. She was no longer an old woman of more than a hundred years, she became a deathless spirit.

I jumped to my feet, throbbing with excitement. She dashed up and caught my hand in a vicelike grip. I had become part of the mad cavalcade.

She ran on, pulling me by her side. I was the living being dragged along by death. I shuddered and wrenched my hand loose from her cold clutch.

She was too wrought up to resume her seat. She continued to move about spasmodically as she spoke:

'On down the road we came – never stopping. On, on, near the city. The other slaves had run down before us and spread the news that dead men were dancing in the master's villa. Crowds filled the roads out from the city. They had heard us coming. They wanted to see with their own eyes. As we bounded around a curve into their midst, they shouted in horror. They had not expected so terrifying a sight. Screaming they turned in their tracks and rushed down the road before us. Like a herd of wild cattle from the hills they stampeded into the city, shoving one another wildly, tripping and falling – all screaming in terror at the oncoming spectacle. Such confusion, fright and horror as no one could picture.

'On in the city we came, heralded by the crazed multitude. Old men throwing away their crutches and running lamely away. Mothers with babies clutched to their breasts, fleeing as if from death itself. The very animals in the town were overcome with terror. Droves of burros charged wildly around the Champ de Mars; horses, deserted by their drivers, crashed their empty carriages against the palms as the crazed beasts sought to escape the tumult. Goats, dogs and fowls sensed the terror and added their voices to the bedlam of the humans. Still on, on, I was dragged. I was as powerless as a baby in that grip of death. Those long strong bones that had only a few hours before been the hand of my lover jerked me along as if I were one of the rags that fluttered behind the crazed spirits.

'My whole soul had gone out in horror. I thought there was no feeling left in me. Drained by terror as I was, I saw before me a sight that seemed to draw all the horror of the fear-stricken city into my own breast. Directly in front of me were the gates to the cemetery!

'The spirits' screams grew wilder and louder than ever. There seemed a note of triumph to the din as I was whisked through the gate.

'On over the graves we went. My mouth was open wide but no sound came. My eyes felt as if they had fallen on my cheeks; my throat as if it were being clutched by the ghosts of the countless dead as I was yanked from one grave to another.

'With one last effort I tore at the bones around my hand. It was like tearing at the marble tombstones. My eyes could see no more. They closed.

'My body swung through the air and bounded over the ground like this – ' The old woman hurtled herself on the grass, turning over several times.

I rushed to her side. It was a violent jolt to an old woman of her years. But she lay there as she fell and continued talking. Spellbound I drank in every word.

'*Oui, Monsieur*, I lay like this. I do not know how long and then I noticed that the cries seemed far away – and different. They were the cries from the frightened city, not the wailing screams of the spirits. I lifted my right hand – it was free. I opened my eyes. There beside me were the bodies, perfectly still, lying peacefully on their backs all in a row. That which had once been Tresaint was nearest me. I reached out fearfully and touched the hand. It was stiff in death.

'I staggered over the graves and out through the cemetery. Some of the braver of the town people did not run when they saw me approaching. They knew that the spirits' shrieks had ceased and that I was alive. They went into the cemetery, on back into the corner where the bodies lay.

'As they lifted up the corpses they discovered a curious looseness to the earth. There were six graves under the covering of sod. Each body had lain evenly over a waiting grave. The spirits had known that, *Monsieur*, and that is why they had rushed down the mountain to set themselves at rest, to release themselves from the dead bodies. That which was Tresaint had tried to drag me to the grave with him, but when he found only the six graves he had flung me aside. There would have been seven graves in the cemetery yonder at the foot of the mountain if I had eaten of the salt.

'Ah! If Tresaint had listened to my warnings my lover would be with me now.'

'But the salt, Marie?' I enquired. 'By obeying the master – is that what keeps you well and strong?'

'What else could it be?' she answered earnestly. 'As surely as the rains come from the sea, if I never tasted salt I should live to be as old as the mountains and as strong.'

'Then you will never die?' I asked, struck by the earnestness in the old woman's voice.

'*Monsieur*, have you a match?'

Wonderingly I made a light as she ran her thin fingers over the grass near her head.

'Would you taste this for me?' She dropped a few grains of salt she had pinched between her fingers into my hand.

I made as if I tasted it. 'It is salt,' I said in a low voice. I was becoming strangely upset – so in sympathy with the old woman's story that I was afraid of a grain of salt.

'Yes,' she said, 'I thought so. That is why I have told you

all this. Everyone who knew my story had died many years ago but now I wanted some one to learn it before I go.'

'But you said you would never go unless you tasted – salt.' I hesitated on the word. My voice was jumpy. The old woman's strange calm and cryptic remarks after her delirious running around the garden had upset me more than I cared to admit.

'Oh! but I have – this afternoon.' Her voice became sharp and venomous. 'That little imp of the Black One threw some in my mouth. He said he stumbled and accidentally a few grains hit my tongue – but,' her voice became low again, 'but what difference does it make how it happened? I have eaten and the curse is upon me. Perhaps a little more will hasten the time.'

She licked her hands hungrily, then ran her tongue over the grass.

I shuddered and rose to my feet.

'Good night, Marie,' I called weakly as I walked to the hotel door.

'*Adieu, Monsieur,*' she answered.

I climbed the stairs to my room. Why did she say farewell instead of good night? I did not want an answer. 'Don't be such a fool,' I told myself, 'as to be worrying over some Voodoo spell of over a hundred years ago.'

I undressed and got into bed, but I could not sleep. I

arose and poured a stiff drink of rum from a bottle on the washstand. With the drink and a cigarette I felt that I could get to sleep. I reached for my matches. Then I remembered I had left them in the garden. The moon had gone down and the night was inky black, but I thought I could find them by locating the stool and feeling around in the grass.

I slipped on my shoes and bathrobe, and groped my way down the back stairs. As I opened the doorI hoped that old Marie had gone to her room. The dark was thick enough to cut with a knife. I hesitated a moment to get my bearings. I did want a cigarette.

Then out straight in front where I was looking I saw a faint glow. She was still there. The glow brightened and the huge bowl of the calabash pipe took shape before my eyes. And then the face! Plainer than in the moonlight!

Great drops of perspiration rolled down my chilled forehead. I was rooted in horror. My heart pounded the roof of my mouth.

That face! The flesh melted away under my terrified gaze. Nothing was left but the grim bones of the dead.

As I watched, stricken with cold terror, old Marie fell headlong on the cool grass of the garden. I knew she was dead, and I knew how it was she had died.

JUMBEE

Henry S. Whitehead

Mr Granville Lee, a Virginian of Virginians, coming out of the World War with a lung wasted and scorched by mustard gas, was recommended by his physician to spend a winter in the spice-and-balm climate of the Lesser Antilles – the lower islands of the West Indian archipelago. He chose one of the American islands, St Croix, the old Santa Cruz – Island of the Holy Cross – named by Columbus himself on his second voyage; once famous for its rum.

It was to Jaffray Da Silva that Mr Lee at last turned for definite information about the local magic; information which, after a two months' residence, accompanied with marked improvement in his general health, he had come to regard as imperative, from the whetting glimpses he had received of its persistence on the island.

Contact with local customs, too, had sufficiently blunted his inherited sensibilities, to make him almost comfortable, as he sat with Mr Da Silva on the cool gallery of that gentleman's beautiful house, in the shade of forty years' growth of bougainvillea, on a certain afternoon. It was the restful gossipy period between five o'clock and dinnertime. A glass jug of foaming rum-swizzel stood on the table between them.

'But, tell me, Mr Da Silva,' he urged, as he absorbed his second glass of the cooling, mild drink, 'have you ever, actually, been confronted with a "*Jumbee*"? – ever really seen one? You say, quite frankly, that you believe in them!'

This was not the first question about *Jumbees* that Mr Lee had asked. He had consulted planters; he had spoken of the matter of *Jumbees* with courteous, intelligent, coloured storekeepers about the town, and even in Christiansted, St Croix's other and larger town on the north side of the island. He had even mentioned the matter to one or two coal-black sugar-field labourers; for he had been on the island just long enough to begin to understand – a little – the weird jargon of speech which Lafcadio Hearn, when he visited St Croix many years before, had not recognised as 'English'.

There had been marked differences in what he had been told. The planters and storekeepers had smiled, though with varying degrees of intensity, and had replied that the Danes had invented *Jumbees*, to keep their estate-labourers indoors after nightfall, thus ensuring a proper night's sleep for them, and minimising the depredations upon growing crops. The labourers whom he had asked, had rolled their eyes somewhat, but, it being broad daylight at the time of the enquiries, they had broken their impassive gravity with smiles, and sought to impress Mr Lee with their lofty contempt for the beliefs of their fellow blacks, and with queerly-phrased assurances that Jumbee is a figment of the imagination.

Nevertheless, Mr Lee was not satisfied. There was something here that he seemed to be missing – something extremely interesting, too, it appeared to him; something very different from 'Bre'r Rabbit' and similar tales of his own remembered childhood in Virginia.

Once, too, he had been reading a book about Martinique and Guadeloupe, those ancient jewels of France's crown, and he had not read far before he met the word '*Zombi*'. After that, he knew, at least, that the Danes had not 'invented' the *Jumbee*. He heard, though vaguely, of the labourer's belief that Sven Garik, who had long ago gone back to his home in Sweden, and Garrity, one of the smaller planters now on the island, were 'wolves'! Lycanthropy, animal-metamorphosis, it appeared, formed part of this strange texture of local belief.

Mr Jaffray Da Silva was one-eighth African. He was, therefore, by island usage, 'coloured', which is as different from being 'black' in the West Indies as anything that can be imagined. Mr Da Silva had been educated in the continental European manner. In his every word and action, he reflected the faultless courtesy of his European forbears. By every right and custom of West Indian society, Mr Da Silva was a coloured gentleman, whose social status was as clear-cut and definite as a cameo.

These islands are largely populated by persons like Mr Da Silva. Despite the difference in their status from what it would be in North America, in the islands it has its advantages – among them that of logic. To the West Indian mind, a man whose heredity is seven-eighths derived from gentry, as like as not with an authentic coats-of-arms, is entitled to be treated accordingly. That is why Mr Da Silva's many clerks, and everybody else who knew him, treated him with deference, addressed him as 'sir', and doffed their hats in continental fashion when meeting; salutes which, of course, Mr Da Silva invariably returned, even to the humblest, which is one of the marks of a gentleman anywhere.

Jaffray Da Silva shifted one thin leg, draped in spotless white drill, over the other, and lit a fresh cigarette.

'Even my friends smile at me, Mr Lee,' he replied, with a tolerant smile, which lightened for an instant his melancholy, ivory-white countenance. 'They laugh at me more or less because I admit I believe in Jumbees. It is possible that everybody with even a small amount of African blood possesses that streak of belief in magic and the like. I seem, though, to have a peculiar aptitude for it! It is a matter of *experience*, with me, sir, and my friends are free to smile at me if they wish. Most of them – well, they do not admit their beliefs as freely as I, perhaps!'

Mr Lee took another sip of the cold swizzel. He had heard how difficult it was to get Jaffray Da Silva to speak of his 'experiences', and he suspected that under his host's even courtesy lay that austere pride which resents anything like ridicule, despite that tolerant smile.

'Please proceed, sir,' urged Mr Lee, and was quite unconscious that he had just used a word which, in his native South, is reserved for gentlemen of pure Caucasian blood.

'When I was a young man,' began Mr Da Silva, 'about 1894, there was a friend of mine named Hilmar Iversen, a Dane, who lived here in the town, up near the Moravian Church on what the people call "Foun'-Out Hill." Iversen had a position under the government, a clerk's job, and his office was in the Fort. On his way home he used to stop here almost every afternoon for a swizzel and a chat. We were great friends, close friends. He was then a man a little past fifty, a butter tub of a fellow, very stout, and, like many of that build, he suffered from heart attacks.

'One night a boy came here for me. It was eleven o'clock, and I was just arranging the mosquito-net on my bed, ready to turn in. The servants had all gone home, so I went to the door myself, in shirt and trousers, and carrying a lamp, to see what was wanted – or, rather, I knew perfectly well what it was – a messenger to tell me Iversen was dead!'

Mr Lee suddenly sat bolt-upright.

'How could you know that?' he enquired, his eyes wide.

Mr Da Silva threw away the remains of his cigarette.

'I sometimes know things like that,' he answered, slowly. 'In this case, Iversen and I had been close friends for years. He and I had talked about magic and that sort of thing a great deal, occult powers, manifestations – that sort of thing. It is a very general topic here, as you may have seen. You would hear more of it if you continued to live here and settled into the ways of the island. In fact, Mr Lee, Iversen and I had made a compact together. The one of us who "went out" first, was to try to warn the other of it. You see, Mr Lee, I had received Iversen's warning less than an hour before.

'I had been sitting out here on the gallery until ten o'clock or so. I was in that very chair you are occupying. Iversen had been having a heart attack. I had been to see him that afternoon. He looked just as he always did when he was recovering from an attack. In fact he intended to return to his office the following morning. Neither of us, I am sure, had given a thought to the possibility of a sudden sinking spell. We had not even referred to our agreement.

'Well, it was about ten, as I've said, when all of a sudden I heard Iversen coming along through the yard below there toward the house along that gravel path. He had, apparently, come through the gate from the Kongensgade – the King Street, as they call it nowadays – and I could hear his heavy step on the gravel very plainly. He had a slight limp. "Heavy crunch-light-crunch; plod-plod – plod-plod"; old Iversen to the life, there was no mistaking his step. There was no moon that night. The half of a waning moon was due to show itself an hour and a half later, but just then it was virtually pitch-black down there in the garden.

'I got up out of my chair and walked over to the top of the steps. To tell you the truth, Mr Lee, I rather suspected – I have a kind of aptitude for that sort of thing – that it was not Iversen himself; how shall I express it? I had the idea from somewhere inside me, that it was Iversen trying to keep our agreement. My instinct assured me that he had just died. I can not tell you how I knew it, but such was the case, Mr Lee.

'So I waited, over there just behind you, at the top of the steps. The footfalls came along steadily. At the foot of the steps, out of the shadow of the hibiscus bushes, it was a trifle less black than farther down the patch. There was a faint illumination, too, from a lamp inside the house. I knew that if it were Iversen, himself, I should be able to see him when the footsteps passed out of the deep shadow of the bushes. I did not speak.

'The footfalls came along toward that point, and passed

it. I strained my eyes through the gloom, and I could see nothing. Then I knew, Mr Lee, that Iversen had died, and that he was keeping his agreement.

'I came back here and sat down in my chair, and waited. The footfalls began to come up the steps. They came along the floor of the gallery, straight toward me. They stopped here, Mr Lee just beside me. I could *feel* Iversen standing here, Mr Lee.' Mr Da Silva pointed to the floor with his slim, rather elegant hand.

'Suddenly, in the dead quiet, I could feel my hair stand up all over my scalp, straight and stiff. The chills started to run down my back, and up again, Mr Lee. I shook like a man with the ague, sitting here in my chair.

'I said: "Iversen, I understand! Iversen, I'm afraid!" My teeth were chattering like castanets, Mr Lee. I said: "Iversen, please go! You have kept the agreement. I am sorry I am afraid, Iversen. The flesh is weak! I am not afraid of *you*, Iversen, old friend. But you will understand, man! It's not ordinary fear. My intellect is all right, Iversen, but I'm badly panic-stricken, so please go, my friend."

'There had been silence, Mr Lee, as I said, before I began to speak to Iversen, for the footsteps had stopped here beside me. But when I said that, and asked my friend to go, I could *feel* that he went at once, and I knew that he had understood how I meant it! It was, suddenly, Mr Lee, as though there had never been any footsteps, if you see what I mean. It is hard to put into words. I daresay, if I had been one of the labourers, I should have been halfway to Christiansted through the estates, Mr Lee, but I was not so frightened that I could not stand my ground.

'After I had recovered myself a little, and my scalp had ceased its prickling, and the chills were no longer running up and down my spine, I rose, and I felt extremely weary, Mr Lee. It had been exhausting. I came into the house and drank a large tot of French brandy, and then I felt better, more like myself. I took my hurricane-lantern and lighted it, and stepped down the path toward the gate leading to the Kongensgade. There was one thing I wished to see down there at the end of the garden. I wanted to see if the gate was fastened, Mr Lee. It was. That huge iron staple, that you noticed, was in place. It has been used to fasten that old gate since some time in the eighteenth century, I imagine. I had not supposed anyone had opened the gate, Mr Lee, but now I knew. There were no footprints in the gravel, Mr Lee. I looked carefully. The marks of the bush-broom where the house-boy had swept the path on his way back from closing the gate were undisturbed, Mr Lee.

'I was satisfied, and no longer even a little frightened. I came back here and sat down, and thought about my long friendship with old Iversen. I felt very sad to know that I should not see him again alive. He would never stop here again afternoons for a swizzel and a chat. About eleven o'clock I went inside the house and was preparing for bed when the rapping came at the front door. You see, Mr Lee, I knew at once what it would mean.

'I went to the door, in shirt and trousers and stocking feet, carrying a lamp. We did not have electric light in those days. At the door stood Iversen's house boy, a young fellow about eighteen. He was half-asleep, and very much upset. He "cut his eyes" at me, and said nothing.

' "What is it, mon?" I asked the boy.

' "Mistress Iversen send ax yo' sir, please come to de house. Mr Iversen die, sir."

' "What time Mr Iversen die, mon – you hear?"

' "I ain' able to say what o'clock, sir. Mistress Iversen come wake me where I sleep in a room in the yard sir, an' sen' me please call you, – I t'ink he die about an hour ago sir."

'I put on my shoes again, and the rest of my clothes, and picked up a St Kitts supplejack – I'll get you one; it's one of those limber, grapevine walking sticks, a handy thing on a dark night – and started with the boy for Iversen's house.

'When we had arrived almost at the Moravian Church, I saw something ahead, near the roadside. It was then about eleven-fifteen, and the streets were deserted. What I saw made me curious to test something. I paused, and told the boy to run on ahead and tell Mrs Iversen I would be there shortly. The boy started to trot ahead. He was pure black, Mr Lee, but he went past what I saw without noticing it. He swerved a little away from it, and I think, perhaps, he slightly quickened his pace just at that point, but that was all.'

'What did you see?' asked Mr Lee, interrupting. He spoke a trifle breathlessly. His left lung was, as yet, far from being healed.

'The Hanging Jumbee,' replied Mr Da Silva, in his usual tones.

'Yes! There at the side of the road were three Jumbees. There's a reference to that in *The History of Stewart McCann*. Perhaps you've run across that, eh?'

Mr Lee nodded, and Mr Da Silva quoted:

'There they hung, though no ladder's rung

Supported their dangling feet.

'And there's another line in *The History*,' he continued, smiling, 'which describes a typical group of Hanging Jumbee:

'Maiden, man-child, and shrew.

'Well, there were the usual three Jumbees, apparently hanging in the air. It wasn't very light, but I could make out a boy of about twelve, a young girl, and a shrivelled old woman – what the author of *The History of Stewart McCann* meant by the word "shrew." He told me himself, by the way, Mr Lee, that he had put feet on his Jumbees mostly for the sake of a convenient rhyme – poetic license! The Hanging Jumbee have no feet. It is one of their peculiarities. Their legs stop at the ankles. They have abnormally long, thin African legs. They are always black, you know. Their feet – if they have them – are always hidden in a kind of mist that lies along the ground wherever one sees them. They shift and "weave", as a full-blooded African does – standing on one foot and resting the other – you've noticed that, of course – or scratching the supporting ankle with the toes of the other foot. They do not swing in the sense that they seem to be swung on a rope – that is not what it means; they do not twirl about. But they do – always – face the oncomer. . . .

'I walked on, slowly, and passed them; and they kept their faces to me as they always do. I'm used to that. . . .

'I went up the steps of the house to the front gallery, and found Mrs Iversen waiting for me. Her sister was with her, too. I remained sitting with them for the best part of an hour. Then two old black women who had been sent for, into the country, arrived. These were two old women who were accustomed to prepare the dead for burial. Then I persuaded the ladies to retire, and started to come home myself.

'It was a little past midnight, perhaps twelve-fifteen. I picked out my own hat from two or three of poor old

Iversen's that were hanging on the rack, took my supplejack, and stepped out of the door onto the little stone gallery at the head of the steps.

'There are about twelve or thirteen steps from the gallery down to the street. As I started down them I noticed a third old black woman sitting, all huddled together, on the bottom step, with her back to me. I thought at once that this must be some old crone who lived with the other two – the preparers of the dead. I imagined that she had been afraid to remain alone in their cabin, and so had accompanied them into the town – they are like children, you know, in some ways – and that, feeling too humble to come into the house, she had sat down to wait on the step and had fallen asleep. You've heard their proverbs, have you not? There's one that exactly fits this situation that I had imagined: "Cockroach no wear crockin' boot when he creep in fowl-house!" It means: "Be very reserved when in the presence of your betters!" Quaint, rather! The poor souls!

'I started to walk down the steps toward the old woman. That scant halfmoon had come up into the sky while I had been sitting with the ladies, and by its light everything was fairly sharply defined. I could see that old woman as plainly as I can see you now, Mr Lee. In fact, I was looking directly at the poor creature as I came down the steps, and fumbling in my pocket for a few coppers for her – for tobacco and sugar, as they say! I was wondering, indeed, why she was not by this time on her feet and making one of their queer little bobbing bows – "cockroach bow to fowl," as they might say! It seemed this old woman must have fallen into a very deep sleep, for she had not moved at all, although ordinarily she would have heard me, for the night was deathly still, and their hearing is extraordinarily acute, like a cat's, or a dog's. I remember that the fragrance from Mrs Iversen's tuberoses in pots on the gallery railing, was pouring out in a stream that night, "making a greeting for the moon!" It was almost overpowering.

'Just as I was putting my foot on the fifth step, there came a tiny little puff of fresh breeze from somewhere in the hills behind Iversen's house. It rustled the dry fronds of a palm-tree that was growing beside the steps. I turned my head in that direction for an instant.

'Mr Lee, when I looked back, down the steps, after what must have been a fifth of a second's inattention, that little old black woman who had been huddled up there on the lowest step, apparently sound asleep, was gone. She had vanished utterly – and, Mr Lee, a little white dog, about the size of a French poodle, was bounding up the steps toward me. With every bound, a step at a leap, the dog increased in size. It seemed to swell out there before my very eyes.

'Then I was really frightened – thoroughly, utterly

frightened. I knew if that animal so much as touched me, it meant death, Mr Lee – absolute, certain death. The little old woman was a "sheen" – *chien*, of course. You know of lycanthropy – wolf-change – of course. Well, this was one of our varieties of it. I do not know what it would be called, I'm sure. "Canicanthropy," perhaps. I don't know, but something – something, first-cousin-once-removed from lycanthropy, and on the downward scale, Mr Lee. The old woman was a were-dog!

'Of course, I had no time to think, only to use my instinct. I swung my supplejack with all my might and brought it down squarely on that beast's head. It was only a step below me then, and I could see the faint moonlight sparkle on the slaver about its mouth. It was then, it seemed to me, about the size of a medium-sized dog – nearly wolf-size, Mr Lee, and a kind of deathly white. I was desperate, and the force with which I struck caused me to lose my balance. I did not fall, but it required a moment or two for me to regain my equilibrium. When I felt my feet firm under me again, I looked about, frantically, on all sides, for the "dog." But it, too, Mr Lee, like the old woman, had quite disappeared. I looked all about, you may well imagine, after that experience, in the clear, thin moonlight. For yards about the foot of the steps, there was no place not even a small nook – where either the "dog" or the old woman could have been concealed. Neither was on the gallery, which was only a few feet square, a mere landing.

'But there came to my ears, sharpened by that night's experiences, from far out among the plantations at the rear of Iversen's house, the pad-pad of naked feet. Someone – something – was running, desperately, off in the direction of the centre of the island, back into the hills, into the deep "bush."

'Then, behind me, out of the house onto the gallery rushed the two old women who had been preparing Iversen's body for its burial. They were enormously excited, and they shouted at me unintelligibly. I will have to render their words for you.

" 'O, de Good Gahd protec' you, Marster Jaffray, sir – de Joombie, de Joombie! De "Sheen," Marster Jaffray! He go, sir?"

'I reassured the poor old souls, and went back home.' Mr Da Silva fell abruptly silent. He slowly shifted his position in his chair, and reached for, and lighted, a fresh cigarette. Mr Lee was absolutely silent. He did not move. Mr Da Silva resumed, deliberately, after obtaining a light.

'You see, Mr Lee, the West Indies are different from any other place in the world, I verily believe, sir. I've said so, anyhow, many a time, although I have never been out of the islands except when I was a young man, to Copenhagen. I've told you exactly what happened that particular night.'

Mr Lee heaved a sigh.

'Thank you, Mr Da Silva, very much indeed, sir,' said he, thoughtfully, and made as though to rise. His service wristwatch indicated six o'clock.

'Let us have a fresh swizzel, at least, before you go,' suggested Mr Da Silva. 'We have a saying here in the island, that a man can't travel on one leg! Perhaps you've heard it already.'

'I have,' said Mr Lee.

'Knud, Knud! You hear, mon? Knud – tell Charlotte to mash up another bal' of ice – you hear? Quickly now,' commanded Mr Da Silva.

I WALKED WITH A ZOMBIE

Inez Wallace

Haiti, that dark island of mystery, where such incredible figures as Christophe, the Black Napoleon, rose to world fame as the Negro emperor, where Voodoo rites link man with the supernatural in a manner beyond understanding – Haiti has yet another phenomenon that baffles the greatest thinkers and scientists of our age.

When I first came to the island and heard the tales I am about to relate, I refused to believe.

I cannot blame you for doubting when you have finished reading this account. Yet, in cold type, placed on the lawbooks of the Republic of Haiti, is official recognition of the existence of a brand of metaphysical magic that is abhorrent beyond words.

Here is the law, found in Article 249 of the Criminal Code of Haiti:

'It shall be qualified as attempted murder the employment which may be made against any person of substances which,

without causing death, produce a lethargic coma more or less prolonged. If, after the administering of such substances, the person has been buried, the act shall be considered murder no matter what result follows.'

In plain words, it is *murder* to bury a person as dead, and afterwards bring that person's body out of the grave to live again – *no matter what result follows.*

That law was put on the books because it has been proved that time and again the mysterious arts of the black people of Haiti have caused dead persons to rise from their graves and enter a soulless existence as slaves, their bodies moving about without any individual intelligence.

These living corpses are called zombies.

They are not ghosts, not phantom wraiths, but flesh and blood bodies which are dead, yet can move, walk, work and sometimes even speak.

The government prefers to say that these people have been drugged and buried, and then dug up again. But that is going a long way around to get out of admitting zombies as a reality.

When I first heard of the zombie, not a word would I listen to without an unbelieving smile. But I have come to look upon the weird legend of the zombie – those dead men and women taken from their graves and made to work by humans – as more than a legend.

I believe because I know from indisputable sources that these things have happened, and are happening today – not many miles from our highly civilised United States, down in the mysterious magic island of Haiti.

For I have heard weird tales from the lips of white men and women whose word I could not doubt, and I have read of zombies in more books than one.

What psychic power can make these dead bodies move, act and walk and dance as if they were alive? And what super-power can even make them talk at times?

From mysterious Haiti come other stories of the occult; mystic tales of voodoo, black magic, spells, hauntings, curses and animal magnetism.

On the dim background of this mysterious island are enacted strange voodoo rites, and the cult of the black he-goat and the white she-goat flourishes even in the most populous Haitian cities. Voodooism is beyond the law, though even the black Emperors of the island practised it and were afraid of voodoo.

But one phenomenon that the natives fear more – and not only the ordinary, ignorant natives, but the cultivated negroes, and also the voodoo doctors who are supposed to be all powerful – is the dread zombie.

For the zombie, and the weird magic that stands behind

him is beyond even the understanding of the voodoo doctors with all their black rites.

And this superstitious fear of the zombie and of those who are familiar with the raising of these dead people is fully justified.

The natives of Haiti maintain that today there are zombies working in the cane fields, around lonely houses on the island, and some say that these mysterious dead workers exist even in the most populated cities. One may know them because, except in rare instances, they never talk, and they stare always straight ahead of them. If one is not certain he will know if he offers the suspected one some salted food, *for the zombie may not taste salt, or he will know at once that he is dead, and will make his living corpse return to the grave no matter where it is, and no one can stop it!*

Not many years ago there occurred near the famed Haitian city, Port-au-Prince, an incident that brought the zombie to my mind at once. A white man who had fallen on evil days and had come to Haiti under the name of George MacDonough, fell in love with a dusky native girl. His love for her lasted only until a white girl fell in love with him. Then he gave up Gramercie for Dorothy Wilson, and they were married.

But he had not finished with Gramercie, whose fierce primitive jealousy was something to be conjured with. He had not been married a year, when his young wife took mysteriously ill and died. Two nights after her burial her grave was found to be disturbed, but it did not warrant the examination which should have been given it.

Six months later a mysterious story began to trickle down into Port-au-Prince. It was said that on the eerie magic slopes of Morne-au-Diable, near the Dominican border, a band of slaves was suspected of being made up of zombies. The whisper spread and spread, and suddenly a new tense note was added to the story when it got around that a white girl was known to be working in the cane fields up there. George MacDonough heard the story as well as many others of the American colony.

He laughed at first, as his companions had done. But then he began to think of his wife's disturbed grave. It had meant nothing to him then, but now – could there be something to this story? He became nervous and frightened, for he remembered that vengeful Gramercie came from the very district that had sent the weird story to the city!

Acting on a sudden impulse, he had the grave of his wife opened. *It was empty!*

To his horror and despair, he found himself thinking with increasing belief of the weird story that had been whispered around for so many weeks now.

Again he took action on impulse, and went into the

interior toward Morne-au-Diable, taking with him a trusted negro guide and two friends. He went secretly in the night, and no word of his expedition got about. His coming upon Gramercie's cane fields was a complete surprise to his former dusky sweetheart.

But the shocking sight he saw in her fields sent madness into his heart, and Gramercie went shrieking with terror into the jungle tracts to escape his vengeance. *For in the fields, working with the negro slaves, was the corpse of George MacDonough's wife!* Before his arrival, Gramercie, hidden by the tall canes, had been making weird passes in the air.

He went up to her, but her blue eyes stared at him blankly. They showed no recognition of her husband.

He understood at last, when his repeated cries brought no response from her, and in the dead of night he took her living-dead body home with him. And again in the dead of night, he took her to the cemetery, opened her grave, gave her salt to eat, and saw her fall, now truly dead, at his feet.

Then George MacDonough sought out Gramercie, but he was too late to take vengeance upon her, for the natives, who fear the zombie and those who put these men and women to work more than the white people, had heard of her crime, and before MacDonough could get to Morne-au-Diable to kill this witch whose power had used his dead wife's body, her own people had brutally murdered her.

I was told by an elderly man whom I shall call Major Hemingway that any white man who had lived for some time in Haiti and had been in touch with its mysterious native life would hesitate a good long while before denying the existence of the zombie.

'You know,' he said, 'once you're out of Haiti those things come back to you. For someone who's never been there – well, it all sounds pretty steep. Most people have a far back fear of voodoo, for it has cropped up even here in the southern part of our United States. But zombies seem hard for them to get near; but they exist, I know.' He then related the following story to me:

'For a time, during a native uprising, I was stationed in the Morne-au-Diable district – a mountainous country, where the natives are pretty ignorant, and superstitious as only negroes can be. Voodoo flourishes there. One night, a pretty negro girl came secretly to me, and entreated me to help her.

'It seemed that two weeks before, her brother had died and had been duly buried, and now she claimed to have seen him working about the house of one Ti Michel, a farmer in his own small way who lived not far from where I was stationed.

'I had heard of the spells and curses of voodoo, and had come to believe them, but this was something new.

'I said, "What can I do?"

'She smiled mysteriously, and handed me a packet of candy – a sort of taffy-like mixture. "Tomorrow," she said, "you go by Ti Michel. In fields you see men working – cane fields. Men stare, look straight ahead, no speak. You give candy."

'I said, "What good will candy do?"

'She said, "You give, you see. Candy fixed with salt."

'Well, I was curious enough to go and do as she asked, and I did. Next day I wandered around to old Ti Michel's place, and it struck me that he looked at me pretty suspiciously. I looked around a little, and finally wandered into his cane fields. All the time he watched me like a cat watches a mouse. I edged closer to the row of men hoeing in the fields, and he came after me.

'Then suddenly he was called across the field by his young son, who had gotten into trouble with one of his workers, and I was left not ten feet from two men and three women workers. I went rapidly over to them, spoke to them, touched them. They did not answer, but straightened up at my touch.

'I'll never forget their eyes! It was like looking into an old, used well at night – you get what I mean?

'Well, I gave them the candy, and they took it and began sucking at it. Then Ti Michel came racing towards me; he had seen me give his workers something, and he began shouting, "What you give 'um? What you give 'um?"

'I never got a chance to answer. Those workers suddenly let out a terrible shriek, dropped their tools, and turned suddenly toward the little town near which I was stationed and began to march in single file out of the fields. Ti Michel stared only for a minute – then he began to run the opposite way. He was never seen again – but two weeks later someone reported having found a bloodstained shirt identified as his. These natives have a way of taking care of people like Ti Michel!

'Well, I was more interested in the zombies, and I followed them. They came to the town, and people began screaming and running away. Some of the men of the town began to run in the direction of the cemetery, toward which the zombies were now running as fast as they could go.

'I could not keep up with them, and lost them. When I got to the cemetery I saw a group of half-hysterical negroes digging frantically at five graves – and near the mounds I saw black, shapeless heaps – the zombies now dead for good!

'I don't expect you to believe it, but I saw it.'

The story of the dancing zombies of Port-au-Prince is interesting from the point of view of throwing some light on the weird magic rites which are concerned in raising the dead from the grave to work in the cane fields.

A negro woman, named Bretéche, had been conducting, only a short distance out of Port-au-Prince, a house in which she gave exhibitions in dancing. This woman, fairly well educated, had been known to have connections with the stage at one time in her early life, and for a time she drew some of the white people to her house.

After a while, only the negro element attended, and she began to attract notice by her daring, for she thought nothing of revealing secret voodoo rites from her stage. Suddenly a whisper started the rounds – *La Bretéche had zombies dancing for her!*

An unofficial investigation disclosed the presence on her stage of seven weird figures who danced at her command, followed every inflection of her voice, but without emotional response – solely in an automatic manner. Never once was one of the strange dancers heard to speak. La Bretéche was questioned.

To all questions she answered that she had not committed murder because all her dancers were already dead. She was asked how this could be, and replied that her dancers had once been buried, and she had dug them up with help and now they were helping her.

'What did you do?' she was asked.

'First, I make mud figure, so' – and she showed them rudely how she did it. 'Mud figure, he resemble man, so.

Then I take and give him breath, like this.' She then held up an imaginary mud image and began to breathe upon it, mumbling at the same time a curious sort of ritual under her breath.

Then she looked up and said, 'Then I say "Dance," and show how. Then they dance for me.'

Cultured white people admit the existence of zombies as well as the government. The government, however, fears to concern itself with the psychic angle. In other words, the government of Haiti says:

'Zombies? Yes, they are here, but we cannot explain them. It is part of the mystery of Haiti.'

An official reply, yes. But it fails to convince me that there are not dead men working in the cane fields of Haiti today.

THE COUNTRY OF THE COMERS-BACK

Lafcadio Hearn

Night in all countries brings with it vaguenesses and illusions which terrify certain imaginations – but in the tropics it produces effects peculiarly impressive and peculiarly sinister. Shapes of vegetation that startle even while the sun shines upon them assume, after his setting, a grimness, – a grotesquery, – a suggestiveness for which there is no name. . . . In the North a tree is simply a tree; – here it is a personality that makes itself felt; it has a vague physiognomy, an indefinable *Me;* it is an Individual (with a capital T); it is a Being (with a capital 'B').

From the highwoods, as the moon mounts, fantastic darknesses descend into the roads – black distortions, mockeries, bad dreams, – an endless procession of goblins. Least startling are the shadows flung down by the various forms of palm, because instantly recognisable; – yet these take the semblance of giant fingers opening and closing over the way, or a black crawling of unutterable spiders. . . .

Nevertheless, these phasma seldom alarm the solitary and

belated Bitaco: the darknesses that creep stealthily along the path have no frightful signification for him, – do not appeal to his imagination; – if he suddenly starts and stops and stares, it is not because of such shapes, but because he has perceived two specks of orange light, and is not yet sure whether they are only fire-flies, or the eyes of a trigonocephalus. The spectres of his fancy have nothing in common with those indistinct and monstrous umbrages: what he most fears, next to the deadly serpent, are human witchcrafts. A white rag, an old bone lying in the path, might be a *maléfice* which, if trodden upon, would cause his leg to blacken and swell up to the size of an elephant's limb; an unopened bundle of plantain leaves or of bamboo strippings, dropped by the way-side, might contain the skin of a *Soucouyan*. But the ghastly being who doffs or dons his skin at will – and the zombi – and the *Moun-Mò* – may be quelled or exorcised by prayer; and the lights of shrines, the white gleaming of crosses, continually remind the traveller of his duty to the Powers that save. All along the way there are shrines at intervals, not very far apart: while standing in the radiance of one niche-lamp, you may perhaps discern the glow of the next, if the road be level and straight. They are almost everywhere, – shining along the skirts of the woods, at the entrance of ravines, by the verges of precipices; – there is a cross even upon the summit of the loftiest peak in the island. And the night-

128

walker removes his hat each time his bare feet touch the soft stream of yellow light outpoured from the illuminated shrine of a white Virgin or a white Christ. These are good ghostly company for him; – he salutes them, talks to them, tells them his pains or fears: their blanched faces seem to him full of sympathy; – they appear to cheer him voicelessly as he strides from gloom to gloom, under the goblinry of those woods which tower black as ebony under the stars. . . . And he has other companionship. One of the greatest terrors of darkness in other lands does not exist here after the setting of the sun – the terror of *Silence*. . . . Tropical night is full of voices – extraordinary populations of crickets are trilling; nations of tree-frogs are chanting; the *Cabri-des-bois** or *cra-cra*, almost deafens you with the wheezy bleating sound by which it earned its creole name; birds pipe: everything that bells, ululates, drones, clacks, guggles, joins the enormous chorus; and you fancy you see all the shadows vibrating to the force of this vocal storm. The true life of Nature in the tropics begins with the darkness, ends with the light.

And it is partly, perhaps, because of these conditions that the coming of the dawn does not dissipate all fears of the supernatural. *I ni pè zombi mênm gran'-jou* ('he is afraid of ghosts even in broad daylight') is a phrase which does not sound exaggerated in these latitudes, – not, at least, to anyone knowing something of the conditions of tropical day, in the hush of the woods, the solemn silence of the hills (broken only by torrent voices that cannot make themselves heard at night), even in the amazing luminosity, there is a something apparitional and weird, – something that seems to weigh upon the world like a measureless haunting. So still are all Nature's chambers that a loud utterance jars upon the ear brutally, like a burst of laughter in a sanctuary. With all its luxuriance of colour, with all its violence of light, this tropical day has its ghostliness and its ghosts. Among the people of colour there are many who believe that even at noon – when the boulevards behind the city are most deserted – the zombis will show themselves to solitary loiterers.

Here a doubt occurs to me, – a doubt regarding the precise nature of a word, which I call upon Adou to explain. Adou is the daughter of the kind old capresse from whom I rent my room in this little mountain cottage. The mother is almost precisely the colour of cinnamon; the daughter's complexion is brighter, – the ripe tint of an orange. . . . Adou tells me creole stories and *tim-tim*. Adou knows all about ghosts, and believes in them. So does Adou's extraordinarily tall brother, Yébé, – my guide among the mountains.

'Adou,' I ask, 'what is a zombi?'

The smile that showed Adou's beautiful white teeth has instantly disappeared; and she answers, very seriously, that she has never seen a zombi, and does not want to see one.

'*Moin pa te janmain oui zombi, – pa. 'lè ouè ço moin!*'

'But, Adou, child, I did not ask you whether you ever saw it; – I asked you only to tell me what it is like?' . . .

Adou hesitates a little, and answers:

'*Zombi? Mais ça fai désòde lanuitt, zombi!*'

'Ah! it is Something which "makes disorder at night." ' Still, that is not a satisfactory explanation. 'Is it the spectre of a dead person, Adou? Is it *one who comes back?*'

'*Non, Missié, – non; çé pa ça.*'

'Not that? . . . Then what was it you said the other night when you were afraid to pass the cemetery on an errand, – *ça ou té ka di*, Adou?'

'*Moin té ka di: "Moin pa lé k'allé bò cimétiè-là pa ouappò moun-mò; – moun-mò ké barré moin: moin pa sé pé vini enco."*' (I said, 'I do not want to go by that cemetery because of the dead folk; – the dead folk will bar the way, and I cannot get back again.')

'And you believe that, Adou?'

'Yes, that is what they say . . . And if you go into the cemetery at night you cannot come out again; the dead folk will stop you – *moun-mò ké barré ou'.* . . .

'But are the dead folk zombis, Adou?'

'No; the *moun-mò* are not zombis. The zombis go everywhere: the dead folk remain in the graveyard. . . . Except on the Night of All Souls: then they go to the houses of their people everywhere.'

'Adou, if after the doors and windows were locked and barred you were to see entering your room in the middle of the night, a woman fourteen feet high?' . . .

'Ah! pa pàlé ça!!' . . .

'No; tell me, Adou.'

'Why, yes: that would be a zombi. It is the zombis who make all those noises at night one cannot understand. . . . Or, again, if I were to see a dog that high [she holds her hand about five feet above the floor] coming into our house at night, I would scream: *Mi Zombi!'*

Then it suddenly occurs to Adou that her mother knows something about zombis.

'Ou! Maman!'

'Eti!' answers old Théréza's voice from the little outbuilding where the evening meal is being prepared, over a charcoal furnace, in an earthen canari.

'Missié-là ka mandé save ça ça yé yonne zombi; – vini ti bouin!' . . . The mother laughs, abandons her canari, and comes in to tell me all she knows about the weird word.

'I ni pè zombi' – I find from old Théréza's explanations – is a phrase indefinite as our own vague expressions, 'afraid of ghosts', 'afraid of the dark'. But the word 'zombi' also has special strange meanings. . . . *'Ou passé nans grand chimin lanuitt, épi ou ka ouè gouôs difé, épi plis ou ka vini assou difé-à*

pli ou ka ouè difé-à ka mâché: çé zombi ka fai ça. . . . Eneò, chouval ka passé, – chouval ka ni anni toua patt: ça zombi.' (You pass along the high-road at night, and you see a great fire, and the more you walk to get to it the more it moves away: it is the zombi makes that. . . . Or a horse with only three legs passes you: that is a zombi.)

'How big is the fire that the zombi makes?' I ask.

'It fills the whole road,' answers Théréza: *'li ka rempli toutt chimin-là.* Folk call those fires the Evil Fires, – *mauvai difé;* – and if you follow them they will lead you into chasms, – *ou ké tombé adans labïme'.*

And then she tells me this:

'Baidaux was a mad man of colour who used to live at St Pierre, in the Street of the Precipice. He was not dangerous, – never did any harm; – his sister used to take care of him. And what I am going to relate is true, – *çe zhistouè veritabe!*

'One day Baidaux said to his sister: *"Moin ni yonne yche, va! – ou pa connaitt li!"* (I have a child, ah! – you never saw it!) His sister paid no attention to what he said that day; but the next day he said it again, and the next, and the next, and every day after – so that his sister at last became much apnoyed by it, and used to cry out: *"Ah! mais pé guiole ou, Baidaux! ou fou pou embêté moin conm ça! – ou bien fou!"*. . . . But he tormented her that way for months and for years.

'One evening he went out, and only came home at

midnight leading a child by the hand, – a black child he had found in the street; and he said to his sister: –

' *"Mi yche-là moin mené ba ou! Tou léjou moin té ka di ou moin tini yonne yche: ou pa té 'lè couè, – eh, ben! MI Y!"* ' (Look at the child I have brought you! Every day I have been telling you I had a child: you would not believe me, – very well, LOOK AT HIM!)

'The sister gave one look, and cried out: *"Baidaux, otí ou pouend yche-là?"* . . . For the child was growing taller and taller every moment. . . . And Baidaux, – because he was mad, – kept saying: *"Çé yche-moin! çé yche moin!"* (It is my child!)

'And the sister threw open the shutters and screamed to all the neighbours, – *"Sécou, sécou, sécou! Vini oué ça Baidaux mené ba moin!"* (Help! help! Come see what Baidaux has brought in here!) And the child said to Baidaux: *"Ou ni bonhè ou fou!"* (You are lucky that you are mad!) . . . Then all the neighbours came running in; but they could not see anything: the zombi was gone.'

As I was saying, strange things happen in the hours of daylight here; – and it is of something which walks abroad under the eye of the sun, even at high noontide, that I wish to speak, while the impressions of a journey one morning to the scene of its last alleged appearance yet remain vivid in my mind.

You follow the mountain road leading from Calebasse over

long meadowed levels two thousand feet above the ocean, into the woods of La Couresse, where it begins to descend slowly, through deep green shadowing, by great zigzags. Then, at a turn, you find yourself unexpectedly looking down upon a planted valley, through plumey fronds of arborescent fern. The surface below seems almost like a lake of gold-green water, – especially when long breaths of mountain-wind set the miles of ripening cane a-ripple from verge to verge: the illusion is marred only by the road, fringed with young cocoa palms, which serpentines across the luminous plain. East, west, and north the horizon is almost wholly hidden by surging of hills: those nearest are softly shaped and exquisitely green; above them loftier undulations take hazier verdancy and darker shadows; farther yet rise silhouettes of blue or violet tone, with one beautiful breast-shaped peak thrusting up in the midst; – vapourous huddling of prodigious shapes – wrinkled, fissured, horned, fantastically tall. . . . Such at least are the colours of the morning. . . . Here and there, between gaps in the volcanic chain, the land hollows into gorges, slopes down into ravines; and the sea's vast disc of turquoise flames up through the interval. Southwardly those deep woods, through which the way winds down, shut in the view. . . . You do not see the plantation buildings till you have advanced some distance into the valley; – they are hidden by a fold of the land, and stand in a little hollow where the road turns; a great quadrangle of low grey antiquated edifices, heavily walled and buttressed, and roofed with red tiles. The court they form opens upon the main route by an immense archway. Farther along ajoupas begin to line the way, – the dwellings of the field hands, – tiny cottages built with trunks of the arborescent fern or with stems of bamboo, and thatched with cane-straw: each in a little garden planted with bananas, yams, couscous, camanioc, choux-caraibes, or other things, – and hedged about with roseaux d'Inde and various flowering shrubs.

Thereafter, only the high whispering wildernesses of cane on either side, – the white silent road winding between its swaying cocoa trees, – and the tips of hills that seem to glide on before you as you walk, and that take, with the deepening of the afternoon light, such amethystine colour as if they were going to become transparent.

It is a breezeless and cloudless noon. Under the dazzling downpour of light the hills seem to smoke blue: something like a thin yellow fog haloes the leagues of ripening cane, – a vast reflection. There is no stir in all the green mysterious front of the vine-veiled woods. The palms of the roads keep their heads quite still, as if listening. The canes do not utter a single susurration. Rarely is there such absolute stillness among them; upon the calmest days there are usually rustlings audible, thin cracklings, faint creepings: sounds that betray the passing of some little animal or reptile – a rat or a manicou, or a zanoli or couresse, – more often, however, no harmless lizard or snake, but the deadly *fer-de-lance*. Today, all these seem to sleep; and there are no workers among the cane to clear away the weeds – to uproot the *pié-treffe, pié-poule, pié-balai, zhèbe-en-mè;* it is the hour of rest.

A woman is coming along the road, – young, very swarthy, very tall, and barefooted, and black-robed; she wears a high white turban with dark stripes, and a white foulard is thrown about her fine shoulders; she bears no burden, and walks very swiftly and noiselessly . . . Soundless as shadow the motion of all these naked-footed people is. On any quiet mountain-way, full of curves, where you fancy yourself alone, you may often be startled by something you *feel*, rather than hear, behind you, – surd steps, the springy movement of a long lithe body, dumb oscillations of raiment; – and ere you can turn to look, the haunter swiftly passes with creole greeting of *'bonjou'* or *'bonsouè, Missié.'* This sudden 'becoming aware' in broad daylight of a living presence unseen is even more disquieting than that sensation which, in absolute darkness, makes one halt all breathlessly before great solid objects, whose proximity has been revealed by some mute blind emanation of force alone. But it is very seldom, indeed, that the negro or half-breed is thus surprised: he seems to divine an advent by some specialised sense, – like an animal – and to become conscious of a look directed upon him from any distance or from behind any covert; – to pass within the range of his keen vision unnoticed is almost impossible. . . . And the approach of this woman has been already observed by the habitants of the ajoupas; – dark faces peer out from windows and doorways; – one half-nude labourer even strolls out to the road-side under the sun to watch her coming. He looks a moment, turns to the hut again, and calls: –

'*Ou-ou! Fafa!*'

'*Étí! Gabou!*'

'*Vini ti bouin! – mi bel négresse!*'

Out rushes Fafa, with his huge straw hat in his hand: '*Otí, Gabou?*'

'*Mi!*'

'*Ah! quimbé moin!*' cries black Fafa, enthusiastically; '*fouinq! li bel! – Jésis-Maīa! li doux!*' . . . Neither ever saw that woman before; and both feel as if they could watch her forever.

There is something superb in the port of a tall young mountain-griffone, or negress, who is comely and knows that she is comely: it is a black poem of artless dignity, primitive grace, savage exultation of movement. . . . '*Ou marché tête enlai conm couresse qui ka passé lariviè*' (You walk with your head in the air, like the couresse-serpent swimming a river) is a creole comparison which pictures perfectly the poise of her neck and chin. And in her walk there is also a serpentine elegance, a sinuous charm: the shoulders do not swing; the cambered torso seems immobile; – but alternately from waist to heel, and from heel to waist, with each long full stride, an indescribable undulation seems to pass; while the folds of her loose robe oscillate to right and left behind her, in perfect libration, with the free swaying of the hips. With us, only a finely trained dancer could attempt such a walk; – with the Martinique woman of colour it is natural as the tint of her skin; and this allurement of motion unrestrained is most marked in those who have never worn shoes, and are clad lightly as the women of antiquity, – in two very thin and simple garments; – chemise and *robe d' indienne.* . . . But whence is she? – of what canton? Not from Vauclin, nor from Lamentin, nor from Marigot, – from Case-Pilote or from Case-Navire: Fafa knows all the people there. Never of Sainte-Anne, nor of Sainte-Luce, nor of Sainte-Marie, nor of Diamant, nor of Gros-Morne, nor of Carbet, – the birthplace of Gabou. Neither is she of the village of the Abysms, which is in the Parish of the Preacher, – nor yet of Ducos nor of François, which are in the Commune of the Holy Ghost. . . .

She approaches the ajoupa: both men remove their big straw hats; and both salute her with a simultaneous *'Bonjou, Manzell.'*

'Bonjou, Missié,' she responds, in a sonorous alto, without

appearing to notice Gabou, – but smiling upon Fafa as she passes, with her great eyes turned full upon his face. . . . All the libertine blood of the man flames under that look; – he feels as if momentarily wrapped in a blaze of black lightning.

'Ça ka fai moin pè,' exclaims Gabou, turning his face towards the ajoupa. Something indefinable in the gaze of the stranger has terrified him.

'Pa ka fai moin pè – fouing!' (She does not make me afraid) laughs Fafa, boldly following her with a smiling swagger.

'Fafa!' cries Gabou, in alarm. *'Fafa, pa fai ça!'*

But Fafa does not heed. The strange woman has slackened her pace, as if inviting pursuit; – another moment and he is at her side.

*'Oti ou ka rété, chè?' he demands, with the boldness of one who knows himself a fine specimen of his race.

*'Zaffai cabritt pa zaffai lapin,' she answers, mockingly.

'Mais pouki ou rhabillé toutt nouè conm ça.'

'Moin pàté deil pou name moin mò.'

'Aïe ya yaïe! . . . Non, vouè! – ca ou kallé atouèlement?'

'Lanmou pàti: moin pàti deīé lanmou.'

'Ho! – ou ni guêpe, anh?'

'Zanoli bail yon bal; épi maboya rentré ladans.'

'Di moin oti ou kallé, doudoux?'

'Jouq lariviè Lezà.'

'*Fouinq! – ni plis passé trente kilomett!*'
'*Eh ben? – ess ou 'lè vini épi moin?*'*

And as she puts the question she stands still and gazes at him; – her voice is no longer mocking: it has taken another tone, – a tone soft as the long golden note of the little brown bird they call the *siffleur-de-montagne*, the mountain-whistler. . . . Yet Fafa hesitates. He hears the clear clang of the plantation bell recalling him to duty; – he sees far down the road – (*Ouill!* how fast they have been walking!) – a white and black speck in the sun: Gabou, uttering through his joined hollowed hands, as through a horn, the *ouklé*, the rally call. For an instant he thinks of the overseer's anger, – of the distance, – of the white road glaring in the dead heat: then he looks again into the black eyes of the strange woman, and answers: '*Oui; – moin ké vini épi ou.*'

With a burst of mischievous laughter, in which Fafa joins, she walks on, – Fafa striding at her side. . . . And Gabou, far off, watches them go, – and wonders that, for the first time since ever they worked together, his comrade failed to answer his *ouklé*.

'*Coument yo ka crié ou, chè?*' asks Fafa, curious to know her name.

'*Châché nom moin ou-menm, duviné.*'

But Fafa never was a good guesser, – never could guess the simplest of tim-tim.

'*Ess Céndrine?*'

'*Non, çé pa ça.*'

'*Ess Vitaline?*'

'*Non, çé pa ça.*'

'*Ess Aza?*'

'*Non, çé pa ça.*'

'*Ess Nini?*'

'*Câché eneo.*'

'*Ess Tité?*'

'*Ou pa save, – tant pis pou ou!*'

'*Ess Youma?*'

'*Pouki ou 'lè save nom moin? – ça ou ké fai épi y?*'

'*Ess Vaiya?*'

'*Non, çé pay.*'

'*Ess Maiyotte?*'

'*Non! ou pa kéjanmain trouvé y!*'

'*Ess Sounoune? – ess Loulouze?*'

She does not answer, but quickens her pace and begins to sing, – not as the half-breed, but as the African sings, – commencing with a low long weird intonation that suddenly breaks into fractions of notes inexpressible, then rising all at once to a liquid purling bird-tone, and descending as abruptly again to the first deep quavering strain:

'*À tè* –
moin ka dòmi toute longue;
Yon paillasse sé fai moin bien,
Doudoux!
À tè –
moin ka dòmi toute longue;
Yon robe biésé séfai moin bien,
Doudoux!
À tè –
moin ka dòmi toute longue;
De jolis foulà sé fai moin bien,
Doudoux!
À tè –
moin ka dòmi toute longue;
Yon joli madras sé fai moin bien,
Doudoux!
À tè –
moin ka dòmi toute longue:
Céàtè . . .'

Obliged from the first to lengthen his stride in order to
keep up with her, Fafa has found his utmost powers of walking
overtaxed, and has been left behind. Already his thin attire
is saturated with sweat, his breathing is almost a panting;
– yet the black bronze of his companion's skin shows no

143

moisture; her rythmic step, her silent respiration, reveal no effort: she laughs at his desperate straining to remain by her side. *'Marché toujou' deié moin, – anh, chè? – marché toujou' deie!'* . . .

And the involuntary laggard – utterly bewitched by the supple allurement of her motion, by the black flame of her gaze, by the savage melody of her chant – wonders more and more who she may be, while she waits for him with her mocking smile.

But Gabou – who has been following and watching from afar off, and sounding his fruitless *ouklé* betimes – suddenly starts, halts, turns, and hurries back, fearfully crossing himself at every step.

He has seen the sign by which She is known. . . .

None ever saw her by night. Her hour is the fullness of the sun's flood-tide; she comes in the dead hush and white flame of windless noons, – when colours appear to take a very unearthliness of intensity, – when even the flash of some colibri, bosomed with living fire, shooting hither and thither among the grenadilla blossoms, seems a spectral happening because of the great green trance of the land. . . .

Mostly she haunts the mountain roads, winding from plantation to plantation, from hamlet to hamlet, – sometimes dominating huge sweeps of azure sea, sometimes shadowed by mornes deep-wooded to the sky. But close to the great towns she sometimes walks: she has been seen at midday upon the highway which overlooks the Cemetery of the Anchorage, behind the cathedral of St Pierre. . . . A black woman, simply clad, of lofty stature and strange beauty, silently standing in the light, *keeping her eyes fixed upon the Sun. . . .*

Day wanes. The further western altitudes shift their pearline grey to deep blue where the sky is yellowed up behind them; and in the darkening hollows of nearer mornes strange shadows gather with the changing of the light – dead indigoes, fuliginous purples, rubifications as of scoriac, – ancient volcanic colours momentarily resurrected by the illusive haze of evening. And the fallow of the canes takes a faint warm ruddy tinge. On certain far high slopes, as the sun lowers, they look like thin golden hairs against the glow, – blond down upon the skin of the living hills.

Still the woman and her follower walk together, – chatting loudly, laughing, chanting snatches of song betimes. And now the valley is well behind them; – they climb the steep road crossing the eastern peaks, – through woods that seem to stifle under burdening of creepers. The shadow of the woman and the shadow of the man, – broadening from their feet, – lengthening prodigiously, – sometimes mixing, fill all the way; sometimes, at a turn, rise up to climb the trees. Huge masses of frondáge, catching the failing light, take strange fiery colour; – the sun's rim almost touches one violet hump in the western procession of volcanic silhouettes. . . .

Sunset, in the tropics, is vaster than sunrise. . . . The dawn, upflaming swiftly from the sea, has no heralding erubescence, no awful blossoming – as in the North: its fairest hues are fawn-colours, dove-tints, and yellows, – pale yellows as of old dead gold, in horizon and flood. But after the mighty heat of day has charged all the blue air with translucent vapour, colours become strangely changed, magnified, transcendentalised when the sun falls once more below the verge of visibility. Nearly an hour before his death, his light begins to turn tint; and all the horizon yellows to the colour of a lemon. Then this hue deepens, through tones of magnificence unspeakable, into orange; and the sea becomes lilac. Orange is the light of the world for a little space; and as the orb sinks, the indigo darkness comes – not descending, but rising, as if from the ground – all within a few minutes. And during those brief minutes peaks and mornes, purpling into richest velvety blackness, appear outlined against passions of fire that rise half-way to the zenith, – enormous furies of vermilion.

The Woman all at once leaves the main road, – begins to mount a steep narrow path leading up from it through the woods upon the left. But Fafa hesitates, – halts a moment to look back. He sees the sun's huge orange face sink down, – sees the weird procession of the peaks vesture themselves in blackness funereal, – sees the burning behind them crimson into awfulness; and a vague fear comes upon him as he looks again up the darkling path to the left. Whither is she now going?

'*Oti ou kallé là?*' he cries.

'*Mais conm ça! – chimin tala plis cou't, – coument?*'

It may be the shortest route, indeed; – but then, the *fer-de-lance!. . . .*

'*Ni sépent ciya, – en pile.*'

No: there is not a single one, she avers; she has taken that path too often not to know:

'*Pa ni sèpent piess! Moin ni coutime passé là; – pa ni piess!*'

She leads the way. . . . Behind them the tremendous glow deepens; – before them the gloom. Enormous gnarled forms of ceiba, balata, acoma, stand dimly revealed as they pass; masses of viney drooping things take, by the failing light, a sanguine tone. For a little while Fafa can plainly discern the figure of the Woman before him; – then, as the path zig-zags into the shadow, he can descry only the white turban and the white foulard; – and then the boughs meet overhead: he can see her no more, and calls to her in alarm:-

'*Oti ou? – moin pa pè ouè arien.*'

Forked pending ends of creepers trail cold across his face.

147

Huge fire-flies sparkle by, – like atoms of kindled charcoal blown by the wind.

'*Içitt! – quimbé lanmain-moin!*' . . .

How cold the hand that guides him! . . . She walks swiftly, surely, as one knowing the path by heart. It zig-zags once more; and the incandescent colour flames again between the trees; – the high vaulting of foliage fissures overhead, revealing the first stars. A *cabritt-bois* begins its chant. They reach the summit of the morne under the clear sky.

The wood is below their feet now; the path curves on eastward between a long swaying of ferns sable in the gloom, – as between a waving of prodigious black feathers. Through the further purpling, loftier altitudes dimly loom; and from some viewless depth, a dull vast rushing sound rises into the night . . . Is it the speech of hurrying waters, or only some tempest of insect voices from those ravines in which the night begins? . . .

Her face is in the darkness as she stands; Fafa's eyes are turned to the iron-crimson of the western sky. He still holds her hand, fondles it, murmurs something to her in undertones.

'*Ess ou ainmein moin conm ça?*' she replies, almost in a whisper.

Oh! yes, yes, yes! . . . more than any living being he loves her! . . . How much? Ever so much, – gouôs conm caze! . . .

Yet she seems to doubt him, – repeating her question over and over: 'Ess ou ainmein moin?'

And all the while – gently, caressingly, imperceptibly, – she draws him a little nearer to the side of the path, nearer to the black waving of the ferns, nearer to the great dull rushing sound that rises from beyond them: – *''Ess ou ainmein moin?'*

'Oui, oui!' he responds, – *'ou save ça! – oui, chè doudoux, ou save ça!!* . . .

And she, suddenly, – turning at once to him and to the last red light, the goblin horror of her face transformed, – shrieks with a burst of hideous laughter: – *'Atò bô!'* (Kiss me now!)

For the fraction of a moment he knows her name: – then, smitten to the brain with the sight of her, reels, recoils, and, backward falling, crashes two thousand feet down to his death upon the rocks of a mountain torrent.

*In creole, *cabritt-bois* ('the Wood-Kid') – a colossal cricket. Precisely at half-past four in the morning it becomes silent; and for thousands of early risers too poor to own a clock, the cessation of its song is the signal to get up.

*'Where are you staying, dear?'

*'Affairs of the goat are not affairs of the rabbit.'

'But why are you dressed all in black like this?

'I wear mourning for my dead soul.'

'Aïe ya yaïe! . . . No, true! . . . where are you going now?'

'Love is gone: I go after love.'

'Ho! you have a Wasp (lover) – eh?'

'The zanoli gives a bait; the *maboya* enters unasked.'

'Tell me where you are going, sweetheart?'

'As far as the River of the Lizard.'

'Fouinq! – that is more than thirty kilometres!'

'What of that? – do you want to come with me?'

THE FLYING HEAD

A Hyatt Verrill

It was indeed strange, Dr Stokes thought, that his Indian labourers should appear so loath to dig into the mound. They worked half-heartedly, hung back, and appeared nervous and ill at ease. Dr Stokes had excavated hundreds of burial mounds in Peru and had disinterred countless Inca and pre-Inca mummies; yet never before had the Cholos showed the least hesitation in digging into graves of their forefathers and dragging out their dessicated bodies.

When the archaeologist questioned them they merely muttered and mumbled in their native Quichua, saying something unintelligible about *supay*, or devil; and when at last the posts and adobe bricks marking a grave were exposed, the men demanded their pay and deserted in a body.

'Looks as if we'd have to do the rest of the work ourselves, Tom,' Dr Stokes said to his assistant.

Presently the last of the bricks were removed, and the scientist uttered an exclamation of delight as he saw the contents of the tomb. The mummy-bundle itself was magnificent with silver and gold ornaments, and grouped about it were splendid specimens of pottery.

'By Jove!' he cried as he examined one of the jars. 'An entirely new motif! See here, Tom!'

Painted in black and scarlet upon the cream-coloured surface of the jar was a grotesque, winged figure resembling an owl, with a horribly fiendish expression on its almost-human face. Never before had Dr Stokes seen anything like it, and his enthusiasm increased when he discovered that every piece of pottery in the tomb bore the same strange design.

All impatience to learn the contents of the mummy-bundle, the two men took it from the grave and packed up the pottery. Loading their discoveries into their ramshackle car, they started on the long drive to San Isidro where, in the scientist's temporary laboratory, the mummy could be unwrapped. It was late when they arrived, but so anxious was the archaeologist to learn what might be hidden under the wrappings of the mummy, that he could not wait until morning and Tom's assistance before getting at it.

With notebook at hand he began removing the layers of coarse cotton cloth, and his enthusiasm increased at the splendid robes and ornate decorations revealed beneath. Never had he seen anything to equal it! Carefully removing and labelling each of the many gold and silver ornaments, folding the delicate robes and making copious notes, Dr Stokes chuckled with delight at the chased silver mask covering the face of the false head, and mentally preened himself on the turquoise and lapis lazuli beads.

Then, as he lifted the last of the gorgeous robes, an ejaculation of wonder came from the scientist's lips. Resting between the drawn-up knees of the mummy, and clasped in the shrunken hands, was a human head.

'By Jove!' Dr Stokes exclaimed. 'A trophy head, and a marvellously fine one at that!'

Triumphant at having made such a remarkable discovery, he stood gazing admiringly at it. The head was perfectly preserved and the eyes, apparently of some dull green, jade-like material, which had been inserted in the sockets, gave a most lifelike effect. On either side of the skull, long black hair hung from beneath a tightly fitting leather cap with long ears or tabs, and this together with the snaky locks and cold, green staring eyes, lent the mummified head a most horrible and fiendish expression. An expression of unspeakable malevolence and cruelty!

'Whoever you were, you were no beauty,' Dr Stokes muttered to himself a little grimly. 'But you're a wonderful specimen, all the same.'

Then, as he carefully moved the mummy's shrivelled hands and lifted the head, preparatory to placing it in a case, the scientist almost dropped the gruesome thing in his sudden astonishment. He stood there staring incredulously, dumbfounded with wonder. Attached to the fearsome head was a tiny, shrivelled body! A body no larger than that of a newly born infant, but unspeakably repulsive with its covering of dark, curly hair.

For a brief instant, his first astonishment over, Dr Stokes thought that the dried body was that of a monkey attached to the trophy head as a decoration; but only a glance was needed to prove this surmise wrong. The body belonged to the head itself. It was the mummy of a strange, horrible freak; a being with the body of a hairy midget, barely a foot in length and with the head of a full-grown man!

Here, indeed, was a momentous discovery. Very carefully placing the unique specimen in a covered tray upon his laboratory table, Dr Stokes switched out the lights and went to his bedroom, highly elated at the results of his latest excavations.

He was not a nervous or excitable man, and through years of disinterring and handling the earthly remains of human beings he had come to regard bones and mummies merely as specimens. He was not addicted to day-dreaming, and there was not a trace of superstition in his makeup. Otherwise his rest might have been disturbed by most unpleasant dreams; but as it was, he slept soundly until suddenly he found himself awake, fully conscious, listening for some sound which he felt sure had awakened him. Then he heard it. A rustling, scratching noise from his laboratory, followed an instant later by a crash.

'Confound those cats!' the scientist exclaimed, leaping from his bed. 'Now one of the beasts has upset something.'

Switching on the lights he glanced about him. Upon the table was the overturned tray, the mummy of the freak beside it, and on the floor was the cover where it had fallen.

'Damn!' Dr Stokes exclaimed aloud. Then, to himself, 'Lucky it wasn't the mummy the beast knocked off. Strange I should have forgotten to close the shutters.'

Replacing the mummy in the tray, he set it upon a shelf; then armed himself with a stout stick and commenced a hunt for the offending feline. But he could find no trace of a trespassing cat. Satisfied that the creature had been frightened by the crash of the falling tray and had dashed out through the barred window, he closed the wooden shutters, switched off the light and again went to bed.

He did not know how long he had slept when he was awakened. For an instant there was no sound, nothing to have disturbed his slumbers. Then from the darkness came a soft, swishing, fluttering noise, and he felt a breath of air against his face as if some moving object had passed swiftly by.

'Bat,' was his mental comment, as he fumbled for his flashlight. As the beam stabbed the darkness he caught a glimpse of a shadowy, indistinct form, two feet or more across the wings, as it flitted through the door leading to the laboratory.

'One of those big fruit-bats,' he decided as he rose. 'Probably that's the nuisance that knocked over the tray. I'll finish him in short order.'

But there was no sign of the bat in the laboratory. Deciding that the creature had found a way out through some aperture under the eaves, Dr Stokes resumed his interrupted slumbers and slept soundly until aroused by Tom's knocking on the outer door.

'I'll bet you sat up all night working on that mummy,' Tom said, as Dr Stokes, in dressing gown and slippers, admitted him. 'Still in bed at this hour and you look all ragged out. Really, you shouldn't – '

'You're wrong, Tom,' the other interrupted. 'I went to bed early enough, but I had a bad night. First a dratted cat came in – I'd forgotten to close the shutters in the laboratory; then one of those big fruit-bats, or maybe it was the bat both times. Anyway, cat or bat, the pest made a racket. Knocked over a tray on my table and –

'Great Scott, I'd forgotten you didn't know. Tom, my boy, that mummy we dug up is a most marvellous discovery!

Absolutely unique. Magnificent robes and ornaments – but nothing compared to what was buried with him. Another mummy? Why, the most amazing mummy ever found in Peru! Just wait till you see it.'

Anxious to witness Tom's astonishment and enthusiasm when he saw the dessicated freak, Dr Stokes led the way to the laboratory and reached for the tray in which he had placed the mummified midget during the night. As he was on the point of lifting it down, there was an exclamation of surprise from Tom.

'Oh, I say, that *is* a find! What a magnificent trophy head!'

Dr Stokes wheeled. 'Trophy head?' he cried. 'What – '

His words died on his lips and he stood staring, dumbfounded, incredulous. Resting in the lap of the mummy, just as he had first seen it, was the mummified freak! How had the thing come there? He was positive he had placed it in the tray on the shelf after the trespassing creature of the night had upset it on the table. And he was equally positive he had *not* replaced it in its original position. Was it possible he had walked in his sleep and, while unconscious, had replaced the shrivelled midget in the mummy's lap? Or had the incidents of the night been merely a dream?

But even so, that would not explain the matter; for he had lifted the supposed trophy head from the mummy's lap and had placed it in the tray on his table before he had retired for the night. Yes, he *must* have placed it there in his sleep. That was the logical explanation.

All these thoughts flashed through his brain in a fraction of a second. Then, recovering himself with a bit of an effort, he stepped forward with a simulated chuckle.

'Trophy head!' he exclaimed. 'Just lift it carefully, Tom, and for heaven's sake don't drop it in your amazement.'

Somewhat puzzled, his assistant gingerly lifted the gruesome green-eyed thing, and a long whistle of astonishment came from his lips.

'Good Lord!' he cried. 'It's a freak! Ugh!' He shuddered. 'It's a perfect horror! I'd hate like blazes to see or meet such a nightmarish thing alive. But it's a marvellous specimen – nothing like it in the world, I suppose. But what do you make of it, Doctor? Why was the other chap buried with this hobgoblin in his lap?'

'I think the explanation is simple enough,' replied the scientist. 'The other chap, as you term him, was unquestionably a noble of high rank – his robes and wealth of gold prove that; and undoubtedly the malformed midget was his court jester, as you might term him. According to the accounts of Francisco Pizarro, the conqueror of Peru, and his fellows, dwarfs or hunchbacks or human freaks were quite commonly kept by members of the Inca court. But I believe this is the first ever to be disinterred.'

Tom had replaced the repulsive thing and was examining the other objects take from the grave and mummy-bundle.

'Gosh!' he exclaimed. 'Did you notice the resemblance between these figures on the pottery and that – that beastly midget? See, Doctor, the heads are almost identical; green eyes, hair, painting and all. And the hairy body! All that horrible thing needs is a pair of wings to make the design a perfect likeness.'

'*Hmm.* Yes, there *is* a stiking similarity,' agreed the other. 'Very likely the designs were intended to portray the creature. Somewhat conventionalized, of course. Wings added for symbolism, perhaps; or possibly, in fact I should say probably, the midget was unable to walk – don't see how he could with the immense head and undeveloped legs – and the artist felt he should be given wings to make up for his handicaps. But just look at this robe, Tom, and start cataloguing the items while I get dressed and run over to Joe's for a cup of coffee.'

Throughout the day the two men worked at the specimens, Tom numbering and cataloguing them while Dr Stokes wrote minute descriptions of each. But busily occupied as he was, a corner of his brain was ceaselessly struggling to straighten out the events of the preceding night. He fought to solve the mystery as to why the mummified freak had been in the mummy's lap, in spite of the fact that he distinctly recalled having placed it on the shelf on the other side of the room.

To Dr Stokes the only logical explanation appeared to be that he had walked in his sleep, a thing he had never done in his life before, and with the remarkable midget's mummy on his mind he had placed it where it had been found. Yet this seemingly reasonable solution of the matter did not entirely satisfy him.

As there was no other possible way to account for it he finally dismissed the matter for the time being, while he took time off for a good dinner and a pleasant evening at the home of the *alcalde*, the local mayor. But when he went to bed his thoughts reverted once more to the events of the previous night. But not for long. He was very sleepy. This time he flattered himself that no cats or bats would disturb him, for he had carefully closed and barred the shutters. Presently he was sleeping soundly.

Dr Stokes awoke from a dreamless slumber to find himself tense, expectant, listening. Something, he couldn't say what, made him feel nervous, apprehensive. Could it be, he wondered, that there had been a slight earthquake shock? Then once again he heard it – the same soft rustling sound of the night before! Something was moving about near him, flitting back and forth in the darkness; and an involuntary shudder passed over the scientist.

But the next instant he was himself again. It was only

that confounded fruit-bat, or another one of its tribe. But how the deuce did the thing get in? Probably never went out, Dr Stokes decided. No doubt the beast had its hideout somewhere in the roof and was trying to get out, but found it impossible with the windows shuttered. Well, he would soon put an end to *that* nuisance.

Rising, Dr Stokes fumbled for a stout stick. Grasping the club he snapped on his flashlight and aimed a vicious blow at a flapping shadow. But the weapon swished harmlessly through the air, and the flitting creature vanished in the darkness of the doorway. Intent on knocking the thing down, the scientist shut the door and, flashing his light about the hallway, entered the laboratory and closed the door behind him.

As he did so there was a swish of air past his head. He involuntarily ducked, and the flying creature swept by within an inch of his face. Wheeling, the scientist struck blindly. There was a soft thud, an agonized cry so filled with mingled pain and anger that Dr Stokes shuddered as he heard the thing stiking the floor.

'Got him!' exulted the scientist, and swung the beam of his flashlight in the direction whence had come the sound of the creature's fall. The torch almost dropped from his hand when he staggered back wide-eyed, chills running up and down his spine. On the floor, staring up at him with green eyes ablaze with fiendish fury and hatred, was the horrible mummified freak! The thing was *alive!*

It was impossible, incredible; and for a brief instant Dr Stokes felt that he must be in the grip of a horrible nightmare. He must break this unholy spell! Controlling his shaken nerves with a tremendous effort, the scientist raised his stick for the fatal blow. Keeping his light focused upon the fearsome thing on the floor, he took a step forward.

A scream of abject terror came from the man's lips. He sprang back, the stick clattering from his hand. Chilled with horror he stood there, powerless to move. The awful head with its diminutive hairy body was advancing! With terror clutching at his heart, icy cold, while beads of cold perspiration oozed from his forehead, he stood transfixed, powerless to move as if hypnotized by the harsh, malignant green eyes in that demoniacal skull. Dr Stokes saw the long tabs of the thing's leather cap tremble and – No, *not* the flaps of the cap but wings – soft, leathery wings that were attached to the nightmarish head of the apparition!

Yet even in his mad, helpless terror the scientist noticed with vast relief that one of the thing's batlike wings was injured, torn, and useless, where the stick had struck. And so this spawn of hell, this awful being, this mummified freak that by some supernatural means had come to life, could no longer fly. But it was creeping toward its attacker!

Uttering strange, uncanny, gibbering sounds, its lips drawn back above sharp, pointed teeth, its baleful green eyes fixed upon the scientist, the loathsome, hideous monstrosity was dragging its attenuated body across the floor; pushing itself forward by its shrunken legs, balancing its great head by its batlike wings and tiny hands; moving slowly, inch by inch, but steadily toward the spot where Dr Stokes stood back against the wall, gasping, choking, dumb with utter horror.

He strove with all his will power to move, to escape, but not a muscle responded. If only he could recover his stick, could crush this devilish spawn of the nether world to a shapeless pulp! But the scientist's limbs, his arms were nerveless, limp, incapable of control. Within two feet of where he stood, the stick rested where it had fallen from his shaking hand.

At his feet, the torch lay on the floor, its beam still directed at the malignant, awful monstrosity that was moving nearer and nearer. Dr Stokes, however, was paralyzed, frozen into immobility with hypnotic terror. Yet his brain was active, his mind receptive, functioning sanely enough. Or *was* he sane? he asked himself.

Did the thing actually exist – or was it but the figment of a disordered mind? His common-sense scientific brain told him it could not be real, that a mummy thousands of years old could not be endowed with life, that a semi-human freak could not possess wings and fly. It was too preposterous, too supernatural to be real. Yet Dr Stokes' staring, horror-filled eyes contradicted the arguments in his brain. The awful thing *was* there, and it was alive, and every moment it was dragging its repulsive, fiendish being nearer; a ghastly, demoniacal thing conjured by some black magic back to life.

Nearer and nearer it crept; in the silence of the room, the scraping, shuffling sounds of the thing's movements seemed loud and distinct. It reached the fallen stick and, in a sudden mad fury seized it in its teeth and shook it as a terrier worries a rat, mouthing and growling, biting splinters from the hard, tough wood. Then, dropping the inanimate club, the ghastly thing gathered itself together, bared its needle-pointed teeth and, with a sudden harsh flap of its wings, leaped at the man!

With a shriek of abject terror the scientist came to life and sprang aside. He stepped upon the torch, reeled backward and fell heavily to the floor as the shattered light plunged the room into inky blackness. As he fell he felt the loathsome, horrible thing strike his leg, and there was a sharp stab of pain as the strong keen teeth of the devilish creature bit into his flesh.

Then he was struggling, fighting madly, clawing and striking with his fists at the misshapen, incredible, indescribably vile semi-human monster that clung to him like a leech. Heedless of the frantic blows rained upon it, the thing was crawling, dragging its way across the scientist's chest, closer and closer to his sweating throat and face.

Dr Stokes' clutching hands grasped a leathery wing, only to release their grip as fanglike teeth bit deeply into his wrists. Screaming with deadly fear, he saw the thing's eyes glowing like green fire in the blackness. In the scientist's nostrils was the musty, fetid odour of ancient, ravaged tombs. His tortured nerves gave way at last. Something seemed to snap within his mind and he sank back limp, inert, unconscious . . .

There was no response to Tom's repeated knocking on the doctor's door. Wondering, thinking it most strange that his employer should be out so early or should be sleeping so soundly, and vaguely troubled, the young assistant walked around the house. The bedroom windows were tightly shuttered, but to Tom's surprise the shutters on the laboratory windows were ajar. Raising himself on tiptoe he peered between the iron bars into the room, only to reel back, feeling faint and nauseated at what he had seen.

Lying upon the laboratory floor in a great pool of blood was the body of the scientist, an expression of unspeakable terror in his dead, glassy eyes, his head twisted horribly to one side, exposing a fearful, ragged gash in his throat.

Trembling in every limb, Tom rushed to the office of

the *alcalde* and in scarcely coherent Spanish babbled that Dr Stokes had been brutally murdered. Battering down the heavy doors, the native police, with the *alcalde* and Tom, dashed through the short hallway to the laboratory.

'*Madre de Dios!*' exclaimed the first man to reach the room, and crossed himself. 'What devil's work is this?'

Steeling himself for the effort, Tom bent over the forlorn body of Dr Stokes.

'Some savage wild beast did this,' he declared, his voice shaky. 'It must have entered by the open window. Perhaps it is still here.'

Whipping out their revolvers the police began searching the room, but no trace of another living thing could be found.

The *alcalde* shook his head. 'Strange things happen,' he said in lowered tones. 'The Senor Stokes desecrated the tombs of the ancient ones. Perchance' – he glanced furtively about him – 'perchance it was no beast, no creature of flesh and blood that destroyed him. The *Indios* tell of unholy things, Senor. They tell of captive devils buried with the ancient dead to protect their bodies and their treasures from being disturbed. Perchance – *quien sabe?*'

'Nonsense!' exclaimed Tom. 'You may believe in such occult things, but I don't!'

Involuntarily Tom glanced at the mummy as he spoke.

A half-suppressed ejaculation came from his lips and a cold chill ran along his spine. Resting between the knees of the mummy was the horrible mummified freak, its jade-green eyes cold and expressionless – yet with its dead, shrunken face and lips smeared with a moist, dull red!

Whether the *alcalde* or the police had noticed it, Tom could not tell. He hardly thought so. Stepping forward, breathing hard and holding his nerves under iron control, he gently drew a corner of a robe and covered the horrible, gruesome thing.

Doctor Stokes' mutilated body had been removed and was resting in its casket, awaiting the aeroplane which had been summoned to carry it to Lima, when Tom re-entered the laboratory. Clenching his teeth, summoning all his self-control, mentally cursing himself for a credulous fool, he hastily gathered the robes and ornaments taken from the mummy, flung them over the shrivelled, dessicated monstrosity, covered it with a blanket and, trembling despite himself, loaded the unwieldy bundle in the ramshackle car. Several hours later he returned, the car empty, with an indefinable feeling of vast relief.

Far out in the desert, amid the crumbling ruins of the forgotten pre-Inca city, the mummy again rested in its ancient tomb.

W. B. SEABROOK

William Buehler Seabrook was born in Westminster, Maryland in 1886. He received his education at Mercersburg Academy in Pennsylvania, Roanoke College in Virginia and Newberry College in South Carolina. A few days after graduating, Seabrook walked into the newspaper offices of the *Augusta Chronicle* in Georgia, and talked his way into a job. Within months he went from a reporter to city editor, but in 1908 he abruptly moved to Switzerland, where he studied philosophy and metaphysics at the University of Geneva. After graduating, Seabrook drifted around Europe for nearly two years, and in 1915 he joined the French Army. During World War I, he was gassed at Verdun, and was later awarded the Croix de Guerre.

After the war, in New York, Seabrook made his start as a writer. Under the encouragement of H. L. Mencken, he began to write news and features for a number of syndicates, including *The New York Times, Cosmopolitan, Reader's Digest* and *Vanity Fair*. His career of travel and adventure – for which he would eventually be famed – began in 1924, with a trip to Arabia which later became his first book, *Adventures in Arabia* (1927). Seabrook followed this up with *The Magic Island* (1929), a book about voodoo worshippers in Haiti, and then his infamous *Jungle Ways* (1930), in which he detailed his time spent with West African cannibals, and his experience of sampling human flesh.

In December 1933, Seabrook was committed at his own request to Bloomingdale, a mental institution near New York City, for treatment for acute alcoholism. He remained here for a year, and recounted his experiences in the 1935 non-fiction work, *Asylum*, which became a bestseller. During the late thirties and early forties he published four more novels, before committing suicide by drug overdose in Rhinebeck, New York, shortly before the end of World War II.

W. STANLEY MOSS

Ivan William "Billy" Stanley Moss was born in Yokohama, Japan in 1921. His family survived the Great Kantō earthquake of 1923, before sending Moss to Charterhouse School in England when he was thirteen years old. Following the outbreak of World War II in 1939, he served on the King's Guard at the Court of St. James's, and saw regular of bouts of Churchillian duty at Chequers. In the latter half of the war Moss spent time at the famous villa Tara, in Cairo, and conducted the near-legendary abduction of General Heinrich Kreipe in Crete, for which he received the Military Cross "for outstanding courage and audacity."

Moss' career as a writer began in the fifties, when he produced five books based on his wartime experiences. The most famous of these was *Ill Met by Moonlight* (1950), a bestseller which detailed, amongst other things, the extraordinary kidnapping of Heinrich Kreipe, and was turned into a film seven years later starring Dick Bogarde and David Oxley. He also co-wrote *Gold Is Where You Hide It: What Happened to the Reichsbank Treasure?* (1956), a popular study of what became of the gold accumulated by the Nazis, and a notable short story, 'The Zombie of Alto Parana'. Towards the end of his life, Moss travelled extensively in Antarctica and the Pacific Islands, before settling in Jamaica, where he died.

HENRY S. WHITEHEAD

Henry St. Clair Whitehead was born in New Jersey in 1882. He graduated from Harvard University in 1904, having been in the same class as future American president Franklin D. Roosevelt, and was ordained as a deacon in Episcopal Church in 1912. Between 1921 and 1929 he served as acting archdeacon of the Virgin Islands, where he gathered much of the material he was to use in his speculative fiction. An early correspondent of fellow writer H. P. Lovecraft, Whitehead's stories appeared from 1924 onwards in *Weird Tales* and a number of other pulp magazines. His 1944 collection, *Jumbee and Other Uncanny Tales*, is regarded as a classic of horror literature. Whitehead spent his later life in Dunedin, Florida, and died in 1932, aged 50.

LAFCADIO HEARN

Patrick Lafcadio Hearn was born in Lefkada, Greece in 1850. He was baptized in the Greek Orthodox Church, but in his infancy, his family relocated to Dublin, Ireland, where Hearn attended the Roman Catholic Ushaw College. Neither of these religious faiths stuck, however, and when he was nineteen Hearn went to the United States, where he began to work in journalism. He gained employment as a reporter for the *Cincinnati Daily Enquirer* in 1872, and became known as an investigative yet sensational journalist.

In 1877, Hearn left Cincinnati for New Orleans, where he remained for almost a decade. His writings about the city's unique cultural life, especially its Creole population and distinctive cuisine, were published in magazines such as *Harper's Weekly* and *Scribner's Magazine*. His best-known New Orleans works are *Gombo Zhèbes, Little Dictionary of Creole Proverbs in Six Dialects* (1885), *La Cuisine Créole* (1885), and *Chita: A Memory of Last Island*, a novella first published in *Harper's Monthly* in 1888. Over the decade, Hearn became a much-loved chronicler of the city; today, more books have been written about him than any former resident of New Orleans other than Louis Armstrong.

Between 1887 and 1890, Hearn worked as a correspondent in the West Indies, before settling in Japan, a country that would provide his greatest inspiration. At a time when Japan was largely unknown to Westerners, Hearn became world-famous for his writings on the country. His book *Glimpses of Unfamiliar Japan* (1894) was hugely popular, and in 1896 he began teaching English literature at Tokyo Imperial University. Hearn penned three more books concerned with Japan and Japanese culture. Amongst the best-remembered of these are his collections of Japanese ghost stories and legends, such as *Japanese Fairy Tales* (1898) and *Kwaidan: Stories and Studies of Strange Things* (1903). Kearn died in Tokyo, Japan in 1904, aged 54. His grave is at the Zōshigaya Cemetery in Toshima, Tokyo.

A. HYATT VERRILL

Alpheus Hyatt Verrill was born in 1871. A graduate of Yale University, he wrote on a variety of topics, ranging from natural history and whaling to juvenile adventures and science fiction. Over the course of his career, he produced some 115 books. However, he was probably best known the travelogues he penned while exploring the Americas and the Caribbean. Indeed, American president Theodore Roosevelt once stated that it was Verrill who "really put the West Indies on the map." Of his short fiction, 26 tales were published in well-known pulp magazine *Amazing Stories*, and Verrill was especially known for his writings in the 'lost race' genre.

www.ingramcontent.com/pod-product-compliance
Lightning Source LLC
Chambersburg PA
CBHW060402030726
47497CB00003B/818